Time After Time

A collection of 13 mysterious tales inspired by history

Thalia Press

Thalia Press

Contents

From the Editor   1

A Nose for Mystery   3
By Andrew MacRae

Shipwrecked   18
By Renee Ebert

The Coffin House   32
By Jesse Bethea

The Tips of One's Fingers   50
By Lance Mason

The Four-Minute Man   77
By Tom Barlow

Boy in a Box   96
By Dennis McFadden

The Nightingale Sings No More   120
By Gary R. Bush

The School Girl and The Illusionist   137
By C. C. Guthrie

The Snow Train 159
By Lise McClendon

Woe In the Windy City 176
By Joe Kilgore

The Day the FBI Came to the Door 198
By Ellen Byerrum

Box of Memories 215
By Bruce H. Markuson

Under the Proctor Street Bridge 219
By Michael Bracken

From the Editor

If you love historical mysteries, you are not alone. Well written historical stories can achieve the perfect balance between entertainment and reflection. They offer escape from present day reality while still inviting readers to examine the timeless aspects of being human. To me, that's a great combination — which is one reason why Thalia Press is offering this anthology of 13 mysterious tales inspired by history. As a bonus, this collection of short stories also allows you to sample the work of authors who may be new to you in a single volume. If you find an author whose story you particularly like within these pages, we encourage you to seek out their work as most of the writers in this anthology also have other short stories and novels you may enjoy.

Thalia Press publishes a number of anthologies following this same short fiction approach in order to create an affordable and quick way for you to sample new-to-you authors. We believe the short story is a great medium for evaluating an author's skill without investing the time or money that a longer work can require. Short stories also fit our modern lifestyle because, face it, most of us have shorter attention spans than we used to before the infinite content possibilities of modern technology took over.

A final note: Our thirteen stories span the gamut from the 1660's all the way up to the 1970's. They are organized roughly in chronological order. This means you can start at the front of the book if you enjoy stories set in prior centuries, or check out the last half of the book if you prefer to read about more modern times. Regardless of your approach, I hope you enjoy these stories as much as we did here at Thalia Press.

Katy Munger, Editor

A Nose for Mystery

By Andrew MacRae

Paris, 1641

A SLOW NIGHT WATCH at la Porte del Montmartre, one of the city's many gates, was interrupted by the arrival of a man whose cape and broad, white-plumed hat identified him as a member of the King's Musketeers. His wide steps and easy confidence belied an age of no more than two and twenty years. The two soldiers on duty, Master Sergeant Jean-Pierre and young private Gaston, snapped to attention on his approach.

"Bonsoir, good sir!" hailed the sergeant with glad recognition of the man approaching them. Private Gaston did not speak but stood at attention with his mouth agape and his eyes wide.

"Good evening, Sergeant. I see I have beaten curfew yet again," the newcomer replied with a good-natured tone. But his voice acquired the touch of sharp-edged steel as he turned to the private.

"Is there something amiss, Private?"

The private still stared, entranced, until Sergeant Jean-Pierre poked him in the ribs with a sharp elbow.

"No, sir," he stammered while his face turned red.

"I'm relieved to hear it, for I have no time to tarry. Here, take these with my thanks for keeping such a lonely watch." With these words the man dug two coins from his purse and handed them to the soldiers, who accepted them gratefully. Then he called, "Au revoir, my friends," and stalked off into the darkness. The cob nails of his boots sounded on the paving stones while his cape swirled behind him. In a moment he turned a corner and was lost from view with only the sound of his receding footsteps remaining. When even those had faded away, the sergeant turned to his unfortunate partner.

"You witless whelp!" He cuffed the private's ear. "The deadliest swordsman in all of France and you risk insulting him by staring in that way!"

"But Sergeant, his nose... I mean, I had heard that it was large, but..."

"But me no buts! Had you been an officer or a gentleman and worth his time you would be lying on the ground, either dead, dying, or inordinately lucky he was in a forgiving mood and left you only wounded." The sergeant looked in the direction in which the stranger had disappeared. "No one, but no one, gives insult to Cyrano de Bergerac!"

———

THE SUBJECT OF THE sergeant's admiration stalked swiftly through the city's dark and empty streets, chaffing at the lateness of the hour. As if reading his thoughts, church bells throughout Paris — led by the sonorous peals of the bells of Notre Dame from its island in the Seine — chimed the hour of ten and the start of curfew. From a distance he heard massive wood and iron gates closing, walling off the city for the night. Had it not been for his horse throwing a shoe two miles short of the city he would have been on time for his meeting with Cheveau, his loyal manservant. At this meeting, the result of months of intrigue, Cheveau was to deliver to his master hard-won proof of a certain government minister's plotting. Cyrano himself had been on the road a week, ensuring their snare was complete.

It was good to return home to Paris, the Jewel of Europe. Cyrano drew a deep breath as he strode through the streets, savoring the many scents and flavors carried by the night air. The summer thus far had been warm but not so hot as to cause the air to reek with sewage and waste. His harsh footsteps became quiet as cobblestones of the major streets gave way to the packed dirt of the lesser avenues. Cyrano craned his neck up and saw a night sky pocked with stars, shining brightly between multistoried buildings of wattle and daub, crowding the streets and turning them into darkened canyons.

Shouts and cries reached Cyrano's ears as he drew close to Le Coq en Vin, the tavern on the narrow and twisting Rue de Ronsard where he was to meet Cheveau. He quickened his already fast pace, turned a corner, and saw a small group of people clustered on the darkened street under the tavern's sign. Curfew is no barrier to a crowd's curiosity. They moved aside in deference at his approach and Cyrano saw in the light spilling from the tavern windows the body of a man lying on the pavement.

It was Cheveau.

Cyrano knelt beside him. Mme Blanc, the wife of the tavern owner, held Cheveau's head cradled in her lap. She looked up at him with pity on her face. "Oh, Captain de Bergerac, I fear you are too late."

The little man stirred at the sound of his patron's name. His eyes opened but could not focus. "Master, are you there?"

Cyrano drew off his gauntlet and took Cheveau's hand in his. "Yes, my friend. I am here, but woefully tardy and for that I apologize with all my heart."

The dying man summoned his remaining strength. His eyes cleared and fixed on the other's face. "No, my master. It is I who must apologize. I let down my guard for a minute as I left the tavern for a breath of air. Three men, who must have been waiting for such a moment, attacked me. I held my own, until one drew a poniard, slipped behind my guard and did stab me from behind."

Cyrano swore beneath his breath and a murmur passed through the listening crowd, shocked at the perfidy of such a cowardly act.

Cyrano's face darkened as pain wracked Cheveau's body.

"Steady, my old friend. Steady."

Cheveau, clearly moments from death, motioned for Cyrano to lean closer and he whispered his last words.

"Master, they have taken the papers." With that the little man's eyes rolled back and he breathed his last.

Cyrano gripped Cheveau's hand one last time, then laid the dead man's hands across his chest and gently closed Cheveau's eyes. As he performed these last acts for his friend, his attention was drawn to traces of a clay-like soil on Cheveau's tunic and pantaloons. It was of a decidedly lighter hue than the compact soil with which the narrow street was lined. With delicate fingers he pinched some of the substance and held it to his prodigious nose. Then he touched a fingertip to his tongue, considered its taste a moment, and nodded.

Cyrano de Bergerac rose to his full height and let his piercing gaze sweep the gathered crowd. "Whosoever did witness this cowardly act and is willing to stand in court and identify the villains who did commit it, shall be doing our King, justice and myself a great service. On whom may I depend?"

Such was the power of his speech and their respect for his person that several of those assembled answered as one.

"I will."

"As will I!"

"And I." This last was said with quiet firmness by Mme Blanc from where she knelt in the street. She had combed Cheveau's hair with her fingers and straightened his clothes, giving him a dignity in death that he lacked in life. Cyrano looked down at her and his angry visage softened. He removed his feathered hat with a sweep and bowed.

"Madame, women such as you are the beating heart of all that is noble in France."

He straightened, replaced his hat with a flourish and turned again to the crowd.

"In a matter of minutes, the night watch will arrive. See that they receive an accurate accounting of what has happened." He turned to a boy whom he had observed watching him. "You, young sir. Will you grant me a favor?"

The boy's eyes grew wide that the great Cyrano should address him. "Oui, Mon Captain," he stammered. Cyrano reached into his purse and removed a coin and presented it to the boy.

"I need you to deliver a message. Run, young man, run as swiftly as your legs can carry you, to the barracks of the King's Musketeers. You know where that is?"

"I do."

"It is past curfew. Can you slip through the streets without being hindered?"

The boy gave a grin full of crooked teeth. "They haven't caught me yet."

Cyrano laughed. "Good for you, my lad! When you get there, ring the bell, pound the door, raise the alarm, and present my compliments to Captain d'Artagnan. Tell him that I ask him to venture forth with some of his fellow musketeers to the Rue des Gobelins where I shall await them."

"But how shall they find you?"

"Tell d'Artagnan that he shall find me by my mark. Now go!"

The boy took off running down the Rue de Ronsard. Cyrano

made to leave in the opposite direction, but as he did a man touched his arm.

"And you, Captain? What is it that you go to do?"

Cyrano de Bergerac smiled a tight, deadly smile that chilled the onlookers. He drew his rapier, held it up and let the torch light glimmer upon the famous blade. The man who asked the question paled and drew back.

"I go, good sir, to see justice is done." And with that, he turned and ran off into the night with his gleaming sword raised over his head and his cape billowing behind.

IN THE STOREROOM OF a tapestry millhouse on Rue des Gobelins, where the air was filled with the sweet, earthy odor of raw wool, a man dressed all in black but for a white cravat sat in a chair, waiting. Somewhere in the distance, a church clock chimed midnight. A single candle guttered on a nearby desk, flickering from a draft of unknown origin. Its flame, the only source of light in the room, provided scant illumination to the cavernous space. Count de Soisson, for it was none other than that infamous rogue, drummed his fingers on the desk, crossed and uncrossed his legs, and stared at the outside door, willing it to open and put an end to his waiting.

Ten long minutes later his patience was rewarded as the door crashed open and three men hurried inside, with one, after a final look outside, closing it behind them. The candle threatened to extinguish, then regained itself.

The men assembled themselves before the man in black and held their doffed caps in front of them.

"Were you followed?" The count's voice was sharp and curt.

"No, Your Honor. We did as instructed and returned by way of many streets and side alleys."

"And did you retrieve the packet?"

After an exchange of worried looks, the man standing in the middle ventured to speak for them. He reached into his tunic and brought forth a small bundle of papers, tied together with a blue ribbon, which he handed to the man.

"Here they are, M'lord."

The man in black studied their faces. His eyes seemed to pierce their thoughts and extract that which they were loath to admit.

"And?"

Their spokesman looked for support among his companions but found none, for they had managed to move back from their hapless colleague a small, but telling, distance.

"M'lord," the man stammered. "We, that is I, found it necessary to kill the one carrying the papers."

"So?" Again, the cold words cut through the air.

"It is too dangerous for me to continue working here in the mill. I must flee the city or I will be hanged for murder."

"Oh, I doubt very much that you shall hang."

Hope dawned in the man's eyes. "Not hang, M'lord?"

"No, I believe that for low-life vermin such as you, the mallet is the proscribed method of execution. After all, there's no reason to waste good rope on the likes of you, when a simple sledge will do." With that callous remark, the Count turned to the desk, untied the ribbon, and began examining the papers bound within.

Then, as if conjured by magic, a gold coin tumbled out of the darkness overhead and landed on the desk with a ringing chime. As the coin spun and settled, it caught the light from the candle and gleamed as if grateful in response. The man in black and his minions seemed hypnotized by the sight and sound until a boisterous voice called out from the darkness.

"That, sir, should pay for rope enough to hang the four of you!"

The Count de Soisson leapt to his feet and drew his rapier. Four pairs of eyes searched the shadows in vain, not knowing from whence came the voice.

Then came the sound of a creaking rope and the rustle of a cape, and down from the storeroom rafters swung Cyrano de Bergerac, resembling nothing less than an avenging angel swooping down from heaven itself. He landed on the floor with cat-like ease. With one fluid motion he released the rope and drew his rapier.

Cyrano ignored the three ruffians who were sidling toward the door and instead addressed himself to the man in black. He gave a theatrical bow. "Well, Count de Soisson, we meet again."

The count's lips curled. "Bah! My men assured me they had not been followed."

Cyrano's teeth shone white in the candlelight. "Nor were they. I had no need to follow them for I already knew from whence they came and to where they would, like rats seeking their nest, return. I had only to wait for them to lead me to the specific building and room, and, as you see, they were kind enough to oblige me."

"How did you come by this knowledge?"

"It is simple. I followed my nose."

"I fail to understand of what help that ugly, ridiculous appendage of yours could provide."

Cyrano's eyes narrowed. "Count de Soisson, all the effluence in all the sewers of Paris cannot mask your traitorous stench." He pointed his sword at the count. "Now, villain. Do you surrender?"

"Never!" The count drew his sword and set himself en guard facing Cyrano.

"Good! You should know that it shall give me great satisfaction to kill you and cheat the hangman of his fees. Defend thyself if you can, thou cur!" And with those words, Cyrano sprang to the attack.

The count was well trained in the deadly art of dueling, and had bested and killed a score of men in such encounters, but he was no match for the greatest swordsman in all of France. Cyrano played with him as a cat plays with a captive mouse, giving him hope one second, dashing it another. Faster and faster the blades flew. The sound of their clashing filled the room. Perspiration beaded the brow of Count de Soisson and his chest began to heave with effort.

Cyrano, by contrast, was nonchalance made manifest. He affected to yawn at the battle's sharpest moments and once, when the count lost his rapier, Cyrano stepped back and allowed him to regain possession of his blade rather than pressing the advantage, a gallantry his opponent would scarce have offered had the situation been reversed.

The candle flickered wildly and Cyrano cast a quick glance toward the door. As expected, the count's men were slipping away, unwilling to join their master in what looked to be certain death.

Seconds later, the door opened again and the three ruffians filed back in, this time each accompanied by a sword at their back, swords held by members of the King's Musketeers. Their commander, a powerfully built man of thirty years, stepped in and surveyed the ongoing duel with a practiced eye.

Cyrano called to him without missing a beat in the deadly dance in which he and his enemy were engaged. "d'Artagnan, you arrive at an opportune time!"

"How is that, my friend?"

"I am endeavoring to decide if I should take this scoundrel in the heart or in the throat. A touch to the heart would kill him faster than he deserves, but should I skewer him in the throat and let him bleed to death with exquisite slowness, this room would reek of blood for days, something I doubt the mill owner would appreciate."

d'Artagnan replied in the same offhand manner of his friend. "A difficult decision indeed, but one that is no longer yours to make."

"How so?" asked Cyrano, parrying a thrust with ease.

"Cardinal Richelieu wishes the count to be taken alive. He has valuable information that His Eminence is most anxious to obtain." d'Artagnan walked over to the table. He gave a brief examination of the papers, then retied their ribbon and placed the bundle within his tunic.

Cyrano protested. "But he caused the murder of Cheveau! It is my right to take his life in return. I must have satisfaction."

"None the less, Cyrano, I must ask you both to put down your swords."

Seemingly forgotten in the exchange was the count who was growing visibly weaker.

"What say you, Count de Soisson?" asked Cyrano with solicitude. "Would you care to retire from the field?"

"Never!" cried the count, his voice hoarse with fatigue. "I will not be taken alive."

"There, you see?" called Cyrano. "He wants me to kill him. It would be churlish of me to refuse, no?"

"Consider, Cyrano, the favor you would do him by killing him. You know the methods by which the Cardinal's inquisitors work."

Cyrano gave his friend's words some thought, and no sooner had he made his decision than it was done. In an instant he redoubled his efforts, driving the count until his back was pressed against the wall. Then Cyrano lunged with a killing stroke aimed at the count's heart. But at the last moment he changed the course of his blade and sank it deep into the count's shoulder.

The count gave a cry of pain and dropped his sword. Cyrano turned his blade within the wound. "That is for Cheveau," he whispered. The count cried out again, and fainting, fell senseless to the floor.

LATER, IN THE WEE hours of the morning, Cyrano sat at a table with d'Artagnan in the comfortable sanctuary of Le Coq en Vin, sharing a bottle of wine in memory of Cheveau and a mutton pie in consideration of their stomachs. As it was long past curfew, the tavern's windows were shuttered against the night. The door opened only on the arrival of one of d'Artagnan's men, who informed his captain that the Count de Soisson's wound was dressed and he was even then being taken across the Seine to the Palais-Cardinal to await his interrogation. A considerate commander, d'Artagnan invited the young musketeer, with the improbable name of Xavier, to join them at the table. Mme Blanc hurried over with another pewter mug.

Xavier, scarcely eighteen and only six months a musketeer, gladly accepted as he was eager to pose a question that had been gnawing at him.

"If you please, Captain d'Artagnan, what were those marks on the walls you followed that led us to the storeroom? While I can read and write, I did not recognize the script."

His tablemates exchanged smiles and the captain answered. "Those are signs only a Gascon can read, my young friend. Monsieur de Bergerac, though born here in Paris, was raised in Gascogne, which, as you know, is my place of birth as well."

Cyrano raised his drinking cup. "To Gascogne!" d'Artagnan raised his in return. The cups met with a clang and the two men drank.

"But now it is my turn to ask a question," said d'Artagnan as he emptied the last of the bottle into their cups, including a generous portion for Xavier. "How did you know where those ruffians would be? And don't give me any nonsense about following your nose."

"Oh, but I did."

"Did what?"

"I followed my nose, or at least so to speak." Cyrano speared the last bite of mutton pie and placed it on the wooden trencher in front of him. "Did you have an opportunity to notice the light-colored dust on Cheveau's tunic and pantaloons?"

d'Artagnan acknowledged he had not.

"Ah, but I did, and I recognized what it was, after I used my nose to ascertain its odor and my tongue to determine its taste."

"And what did the odor and taste tell you, other than it was dirt?"

"It told me it was fuller's earth."

"Ah, but of course," replied d'Artagnan with sudden understanding.

Young Xavier looked from one to the other, suspecting a joke was being playing upon him. Finally, unable to resist any longer he asked, "What is fuller's earth and why should it be significant?"

It was Cyrano who deigned to reply. "Fuller's earth is a particular type of clay that, when combined with piss, is used by wool workers to remove the oil from raw wool. In all of Paris, there is but one neighborhood where fuller's earth will be found in abundance and that is along the Rue des Gobelins, where the wool and tapestry guilds ply their trade."

d'Artagnan shook his head in amazement at his friend's acumen. "It is no wonder that sly fox, the Cardinal, asked you to take leave from the musketeers and serve as his confidential agent... Ow!" His words were cut off by a sharp look and sharper kick under the table from Cyrano, followed by a quick nod toward their young companion. d'Artagnan attempted to cover up his slip of the tongue by changing the subject. He stood and raised his cup and the others followed suit. "To our king, our country, and to Cyrano de Bergerac, the greatest swordsman in France!"

Cyrano considered before joining them in the toast. Was it proper protocol to drink when the toast honors you? Then he decided he could not deny the truth of it and drank his wine with pleasure.

—THE END—

About the Author

Andrew MacRae is the author of *Murder Misdirected* and *Murder Miscalculated,* two novels that feature a bookstore, a cat, and a former pickpocket who can't help getting into trouble. He also had numerous short stories published, mostly in the crime and science fiction genres, including *The Case of the Murderous Mermaid and Other Stories.*

Shipwrecked

By Renee Ebert

AFTER WE WASHED ASHORE, and after the first shock of the aloneness of it, we set to work surviving. It was good that we both thought alike when it came to trying to keep living. It was bad that Henry was suddenly the person we both knew existed inside the insincere exterior, the man who was a bully with one goal in mind, getting his own way, but not the man he shared with the world.

There are a few things I have forced myself to consider good luck. It was fortunate, for instance, that the bow of the first deck of the Angel Maid was salvaged and washed up along with us. Inside the Captain's quarters there were valuable lifesaving medicines, a logbook with Captain Jackson's last notes, stating a general location of where we were in the event the log survived or our good luck lasted till someone came looking for us. There were some foodstuffs, but most of all there were my plants, and my first quick trip away from the sand I saw the island had fertile, rich volcanic soil.

I will never understand how half of the ship came to rest on that reef. Why weren't any of the shipmates or passengers transported there too? Why only a perfect slice of two decks, intact; captain's logs, the sextant, all of its beautifully polished brass and moving parts survived the waves that pushed the ship toward the reef, the shelf that it landed on? It survived and so did we.

I.

The first shock of the cold sea prompted action, the water inching into the crevices of the ship, creeping up to our cabin, where we sat. Quick action from Henry as he pulled me up out of my chair and dragged me up to the deck. Others like us, men, some women, and children on their way back to their homes in America, were startled into speech, some crying, sailors hollering, officers shouting orders. The sailors and the officers were prepared for this, as they hoisted sails, a man high up in the sails' mast called out "land!" pointing east. We shielded our eyes from the early afternoon sun. All heads turned toward his straightened, raised arm to see a thin line across the horizon. *Yes!* My thoughts shouted out at me, it could be land... or nothing. It could just be nothing. If a mirage of a water line could rest on the sand in a desert, then it might be that a mirage of land laid on the horizon could taunt as easily on the ship's deck.

I turned to hear Henry's voice above the others. "Bring that rope, boy." The cabin boy of ten or eleven ran to Henry best he could with a rope of six inches thick, its weight limiting his progress. "Give it here. Good. Good. Elizabeth, take hold." He wrapped it around me, fighting the jostling crowd that moved up and back with the giant waves pushing our ship like a cork in a bathtub.

"What about you, Henry? Please take care of yourself." I reached out my hand to him, but we both were distracted and turned toward a terrible cracking sound, like dry wood in a fire. It was the great ship breaking in two. Henry pulled us with the rope to where it was tied to a dinghy. How did he know? Grabbing a length of the rope, he wrapped it about himself and pushed me over into the dinghy. He used the rope to retrace his steps, to help others to the safety of the little boat, but they were all windward almost to a tipping point of the ship.

"Hold fast now, girl." His big hands circled my waist as he joined me in the little boat just as it sprung from the side of the ship and jettisoned into the water and away from the ballast point. The terrible cracking continued as the ship sank — and with her, all the others. We were unable to see the hopeless others with waves running higher than city buildings. But Henry saved us. He saved me.

THERE WAS A STORM after the ship went down, the sea in turmoil tumbled out dark and murky water and the dinghy rocked and pitched. The sky had already darkened and with the storm the stars and moonlight were obliterated. Henry wrestled with the ropes still attached to the little boat and secured them around us.

"Good thing we got hold of these tarps," Henry shouted to me over the sound of the wind. They were lightweight canvas which he now fastened around each of us, while I wondered in the back of my mind whether they would become our shrouds.

"Henry. Can you see anyone out there?" I pointed to the high waves farther away and thanked God again for delivering us because I knew Henry's answer as he peered further away, that there were no others who were saved, at least that we could see. I prayed for them all, trying to erase from my mind the women and babies I had seen, spoke to, whose little ones I had held for them while they sought food or the comfort of the women's bathroom. The shudder in me began to grow and Henry saw this, reached to me and rubbed my hands and arms and even pinched my cheeks.

"Elizabeth, you cannot lose consciousness. You must not faint or sleep because we will need all your strength to help us stay afloat." He shouted to me, repeating this refrain, and I sat up abruptly and at attention, knowing we must both be vigilant to save ourselves.

II.

I woke first. Henry must have dozed through exhaustion and shock. The dinghy, caught by southwest winds that pushed it along, brought us to a peaceful bay inlet where the ocean lapped quietly onto a shoreline that arched around in an almost perfect semi-circle. Far down the beach, at the place where the land curved away from us, was a rocky shelf and perched on it was the ship's bow with the upper and second decks. Later we would see it all, the large planks of wood that were shattered like broken bones, reminding me of those horrific daguerreotypes I'd seen, of wounded and dead soldiers from our own Civil War.

III.

How I knew things had changed.

I would like to say it started out well from the time we woke up on the sand of this island, but there was anarchy in attendance even then. The very paper on which I scribble is just one proof of what I am about to reveal. This page and all the writing materials could tell my story for me. The ink I use is hidden from Henry as are the scrolls of paper I steal each time we visit the ship, still sitting fixed on the reef. Henry goes aboard first as we agreed, stepping from the dinghy. I should say, as we came together to agree upon, because it was his decision. A case in point.

"We need a plan, Elizabeth." Henry is puffing on a pipe he filled with tobacco I found on board the ship's second deck.

"A total plan, Henry? Or should we take it in pieces?" I remember my voice was quizzical and to the point. It was met with a fierce slap across my face, from eye to chin, and forced me to my side. Shocked at first, then a riot of anger flooded my mind, my trembling a sign of my rage.

"What is wrong with you?" I held back sobs when I saw his clenched fists waiting to assault me again.

He sits up in front of the fire, preparing to deliver a decree. My mind works quickly to resolve what has just happened. *Survive, I think to myself, survive.* I am not surprised; half a bottle of whiskey consumed, the one item Henry searches for on trips on board the ship.

"The plan." He veers toward me, face-to-face, almost touching. I feel his hot breath of bourbon or rum. "The plan." He says this more loudly. "Is to survive. Fresh water, food, fire. We have all three." His voice trails off, thinking, haphazard thoughts. I know this from hearing him ramble disjointed sentences of nonsense. He congratulates himself for his superior mind. It is clear that he has lost his way to a particular logic. He takes another large drought of the whiskey and loses his balance, leans on his left elbow. Even in the soft sand, he winces, and I know it is either seriously dislocated, or worse, it is broken at the joint which is the most difficult bone to heal and, therefore, he has only his right hand and arm.

I touch my cheek where it burns. Even without a mirror, I know it is swollen. The eyelid feels heavy, telling me that it, too, is thick from trauma and may close. I walk to the cool water drum we rolled to the shade the first day and open the spigot to wet a rag. Henry puffs at his pipe and looks out to sea as I gently press the rag to my eye. *Sight is precious here.* I find I am thinking in fast mental gulps, trying to make sense of the violence. Henry is beginning to turn away from his fascination with the waves lapping onto the shore. I have to reason myself into a peaceful state and sort this all out when I am alone.

"Henry, dear, let me help you. You may have chipped the bone. Your elbow must stay fixed to heal properly." His fear of dying, especially dying slowly, is evident and holds tight to him. He alternates from violence to fear that makes him, for most of the time, less vicious toward me and more vulnerable to himself. My personal fear is of him dying and leaving me all alone here. I try to make sense of what is happening to Henry, to find a way, if there is one, that will heal him in his mind as much as his weakened left arm and elbow. My goal is two-fold: keep Henry alive and restore his sanity.

He has laid back against large palm fronds set up near a volcanic rock, all this while after striking me, thinking — but about what? My first thought is whether he's forgotten but then he speaks.

"Sorry for that little slip back there. Perhaps a bit too much of the whiskey, though a fine blend." Henry refers to the incident as 'back there', the few steps back in time when he assaulted me. His voice is conciliatory, just loud enough to hear over the waves which are growing with the tide coming in. There is irony in his voice. *So, you know what you did!*

"Yes, a plan in pieces, as we said. That makes the most sense." He waits, now, for me to continue sharing my thoughts, so he can claim them for his own. A wise insanity. I straighten my white cotton slip, all corsets removed when we dressed down for this very warm and humid island. Henry wears a pair of linen trousers that I cut to his knees with pinking shears, loose fitting as our diet is not so rich.

"We have clean drinking water from capturing rainwater in canvas tarps and then filling the empty barrels and casks that floated here with us. We use boiled salt water to remove the salt and bathe in and wash our clothes," I hurriedly point out "Thanks to your keen eye, we have matches and a flint should the constant fire be ended by the storms."

I had placed the fire inside of a small and deep cave and tend it often. Yes, in my mind I thank him for his quick thinking that saved us both. That much cannot be denied. But now, and in the last week, in place of a man who knows control of temper, there is a beast. If he were whole, instead of badly crippled, he might be dangerous, but he is confused, forgetting moment to moment.

I woke up late at night after the assault; the moon was down so the dark surrounded us. As I sat up, there was comfort in knowing Henry needed me as much or more on this island.

Need, in any society, is the reason people will be good to one another and not stretch the boundaries of good or civil behavior. Avoiding punishment but also abandonment; not being alone. This stark and stranded life was our reality, so therefore the reason why a man easily persuaded toward rough and violent ways forced himself all those years to harness his natural tendencies. Living in Chicago I was never far away from this truth. Though Henry loved me, our four children, he'd reigned in on the Teddy Roosevelt wildness he championed and was now awakened in him; he was truly possessed by that model of false masculinity.

Tears came to my eyes, though not for the place we inhabit. Instead, I think of my children. Not wanting or willing to indulge myself nor pine for things I could not have, circumstances I cannot change, I had set a task for myself to sort out all that I knew and all that I could have to keep us safe. The medical books and medicines, the plants and, finally, my own sanity.

Much later in the evening after he had struck me, Henry smiled his approval at this last reminder, and reached a tender hand to my chin. This seemed more a real apology than his offhanded obligatory remarks. His memory is in flight as he talks on about organizing, sorting materials, even how to plan a garden, all of which has forced me to see that, at this moment, Henry is not sane because he has watched me these two weeks, accomplishing these tasks while he remained lying back to avoid his injured arm.

"The fire needs tending." Henry uses his right arm and a heavy branch to support himself, avoiding the use of his injured elbow. I continue a quiet internal litany, this time thankful for the ship's two decks perched on the reef. They hold a vital part of our existence and survival.

"I was just thinking how grateful I am to find these medical books. There are instructions here on every conceivable accident where bones are involved, Henry. I've found some drawings for setting your elbow and holding it fixed so it can heal."

Instinctively Henry moves away from me, fear visits him again, of the pain or perhaps disfigurement if I am not successful in setting the bone. I move slowly toward him and open the book as I sit close enough for our bodies to touch. I feel this would be reassuring to him and it seems to work.

"Look at the way they demonstrate with this drawing. The normal position of the arm and elbow." I point to the place and he leans close to see the many drawings.

"I see what you mean, Elizabeth." He looks deeply into my face, searching for the truth of the matter. "What would happen if we left the bone where it is?"

"It will heal but in the wrong way, and you might lose the use of it." I say this gently to soothe over the facts because it is horrible enough in itself. "I've been thinking that we have the captain's medicine chest, where we might find some laudanum for you to take before I set the bone." I know the laudanum is there, but from the first, and before his violent attack on me, I hid it away in my few pieces of clothing. I must think through this fact later, along with Henry's violence, to study my actions so that Henry and I can benefit from these thoughts and the plans that come about because of them. My chief desire is for both of us to survive.

Henry closes his eyes and falls into an easy reverie, awake but transported beyond the warm tropical breeze, maybe back to Chicago where on this late February day the sleet would be falling on the city and country roads, where the dray horses would struggle against the ice. He stirs out of resting.

"I am afraid, Elizabeth, but I know you're right and thank God that we both survived to see this day. I would not want to be here alone, but with you."

"And in all my heart I feel the same. Thank you for trusting me to help you. It won't be quite so bad. Let's have our fish dinner and some of those greens I found that are pictured in the botany books as safe to eat. Then I'll search for that medicine and make you comfortable for sleep after the work has been done." Henry nods in agreement and I build a small fire to quick-fry the fish I'd gutted and cleaned.

He pushes at the fire to stir it up in anticipation of the fish I've kept wrapped in large palm leaves. "It would certainly break the monotony of the meals if we can find other edibles, don't you think?" he asks.

"Something to add to our list, Henry. We can find a safe way to walk around the island, maybe a little farther inland." I take out a scrap of paper from inside the corset cover I wear as a shirt, and with it a pencil stub. The time is perfect for planning "We might find some vegetables saved inside the ship and bring them here to grow." The thought of our being here long enough to harvest food depresses me. It must be the same for Henry. "They can grow fast here with the constant sun and light rains. Don't you think?"

He nods, his face taking on a sad and hopeless look. "I remember tomatoes and some greens, cabbages."

"Now that would be a prize winner for you, Elizabeth." He touches my face again, softer even than the last time. "My sweet Eliza." My plan, forming in pieces now includes a search for something to mollify Henry for when he drinks. A plant that will act as a sleeping powder. I know with surety that Henry will wake in the morning and will become alarmed when he sees the ugly blue and red bruising of my eye. I've already decided to say that I fell on the beach and hit one of the jutting rocks. Whatever sanity that exists in him will want to grab at that as truth rather than what really happened.

"We need a better place to sleep, away from the beach, perhaps we can cut back some of the lower plants and use the tops of the trees as a roof. The canvas tarp hung off them may be a good way, don't you think?"

IV.

The night finally grows peaceful. The tide is low and laps against the shore and lulls Henry deeper into sleep born of his drunken stupor. Like walking into another room, my mind immediately shifted to thinking as I had when I was at Boston College, an academic discipline I am grateful for. My friend Harriet's voice speaks to me as though she is sitting here with me. I use this as my guide to sort out Henry's condition and our survival into our uncertain future.

My brain has never been called upon to be this active. I am thankful each day for little and seemingly insignificant thoughts because I find they lead to much bigger and catastrophic possibilities which I encourage because, as the plans are visualized, I can weigh the advantages and see good or possible bad decisions.

Henry's broken ulna and broken mind are constant reminders of the bigger problems that may lay ahead. I begin now to make my lists. First, I reason that Henry is strong as well as injured. He will survive my fixing his elbow. Against this are his tempers which sway and switch directions like the breezes. Violent one moment, soft and caring another. There is a part of him that is devious, that plays with my mind as he did after his attack. I automatically reach carefully for my eye.

Out of a caution deep inside me that directed my actions, I have sequestered some of our provisions to another side of the place where we are camped. I wanted to protect the medical books I found in the captain's rooms because I sensed I might need them and hid them because Henry had begun to exhibit erratic behavior from the time of his injury. Are the two things connected?

Two nights pass. Turning the pages of the heavy books with bright moonlight as my lamp, I attempt to find a connection. There is one note suggesting that pain from a bone break can cause erratic behavior. That is not difficult to believe, as I've seen Henry's pain and his personality altering together. I've dispensed with questioning the logic of this and find myself believing only what I observe as there are no guides, nor experts here, to form my thoughts nor contradict my own conclusions. This does not trouble me. In fact, I find it refreshing, and once again I am drawn to the voice of my practical and smart friend, Harriet. She would delight in these discoveries of mine.

"Elizabeth, you are so accomplished, you read people so easily, find their foibles, the ones they try to hide the most and you pick them out like stars in a clear night sky." Harriet said this to me in our first year at Boston College.

V.

In the quieter times I can reflect, and I find I have to work at not becoming emotional about our situation. When I am busier, it's easy to fall into the rhythm of the task at hand. Not so when I have leisure. I find that if I organize everything, there is an ebb and flow, much like the ocean that laps against the shore in this little bay. I liken it to the stormier ocean that crashes against the rocky areas in opposition to this more peaceful side of the island.

It is during this time that I allow myself thoughts of my four children. Memories beckon that could easily strand me in a weeping puddle, but then what good would that do for me or for Henry?

Now, with Henry napping after a big lunch of fish and some of the island's edible plants, I can think of Foster, my youngest son, and send messages to him in my mind, things I would say if I were safely and miraculously delivered back home.

I tell those of you who may read this log many years from now, that I have two sons and two daughters. All are grown and the youngest, Foster is twenty years old. I think of him as having one foot into manhood, the other struggling to catch up. He is Henry's least favorite, and therefore the one I seek to protect.

The year is 1882 and we got here by chance by joining an expedition to the Galapagos Islands that I was enchanted with. I remember how Henry finally capitulated, or perhaps caught my enthusiasm for exploring something foreign, exotic, and a little dangerous. And now? Now we just survive.

—THE END—

About the Author

Renee Ebert studied English literature and philosophy at Georgetown University and holds a master's degree from UCLA. She works in philanthropy to support marginalized populations in the U.S. and internationally. Her writing has been featured in the U.S., Canada, and the U.K. in the anthology *In The Company of Women, Backchannels Journal, The Woolf* literary magazine (London), *CommuterLit* (Toronto), and two novels — *Until the Darkness Goes* and *Dead Eyes in Late Summer* — as well as many other publications. She was a finalist for Bellingham Review's 2021 Tobias Wolff Award for Fiction as well as the Bridport Poetry Prize (Dorset, U.K.). Learn more at rebertnovels.com or look for her on Facebook, X, and Goodreads.

The Coffin House

By Jesse Bethea

HIGH STREET WAS A ramrod straight river of mud and slush, and it mattered not at all to the black coach tearing through Columbus in the icy rain. Pulled by a team of four angry horses, the coach turned sharply into Hickory Alley. There, Eileen Monahan stood waiting in the doorway of her father's darkened butcher shop.

She was sixteen then, fair-haired and freckled, clutching a knit shawl over her shoulders that did little to keep out the soggy, winter cold. It was nearly Christmas, and the Prussian family in the building across the alley were singing.

"Stille nacht... Heilige nacht..."

The girl shivered as the terrifying coach stopped in front of her. The tired horses sent up clouds of white steam as she climbed inside.

Slamming the door shut, she looked across the small space at the shadowed figure sitting opposite. Neither said anything at first. They listened to the heavy, icy raindrops plucking away at the roof of the coach. Finally, the woman who owned the coach stirred.

"You signaled," sighed Ms. Charlotte.

The only part of her Eileen could see clearly was an ear, softly illuminated by a single streetlamp, blurred by rain streaming down the coach windows.

Eileen nodded. She had tied the black ribbon on the North Graveyard fencepost that afternoon.

"Well," said Ms. Charlotte. "Explain yourself. What did you hear?"

"He came," said Eileen. "The man you asked after. He arrived at the camp this morning."

In the weak gaslight, Eileen could see the woman was nodding. "Robert Creighton."

"He's a lieutenant in the First Alabama Infantry."

"He's no lieutenant," scoffed Ms. Charlotte. "He's never been to Alabama in his life, and his real name is certainly not Robert Creighton."

Eileen knew better than to ask how Ms. Charlotte knew such things. The lady owned many pairs of ears. "When they brought him to the camp, they said he was a raider. Came up north with John Hunt Morgan."

"The raiders were all captured months ago, along with Morgan," said Ms. Charlotte. "And when the traitorous toad tunneled himself out of prison, he didn't even bother to save his own enlisted men."

"Apparently Robert Creighton escaped capture," said Eileen. "Hid out in the woods down around Marietta."

"An obvious fiction," said Ms. Charlotte. "He was captured because he wanted to be. He is at Camp Chase because he wants to be. Has our mutual friend taken any special interest in the young man? Come now, girl, I don't pay you to stay tight-lipped."

Ms. Charlotte refused to call Ms. Coffin by any name other than "our mutual friend."

"I haven't noticed any special interest, ma'am," said Eileen. "I keep an eye on her all the time I'm there, but we've got lots of wounded and even more sick. Lots of boys to take care of."

The woman scoffed. "*Boys.* Our boys or theirs?"

"We take care of 'em both, ma'am," said Eileen.

But it was a prison camp. She spent much more time tending to sick and wounded rebels than federals.

Ms. Charlotte scoffed again. "Traitors, the lot of them. The rebels, Mr. Creighton — but worst of all, our mutual friend."

Eileen squirmed in the coach seat. "But how can you know that your sis...I mean...how do you know Ms. Coffin is a traitor?"

Eileen shivered as she imagined the icy glare Ms. Charlotte was probably sending her through the darkness. So viciously did the woman hate her own sister that she refused to even say the word.

"I am certain," said Ms. Charlotte. "I have always been certain. She has charmed everyone in this city, but I see through it all."

The shadow across from Eileen shifted and seemed to stare through the window for quite a long moment. "No, I am certain. I have my sources, young lady. Robert Creighton needs to deliver a message — this much I know. He wanted to be captured. He wanted to be sent to Camp Chase. He will approach her or she will approach him. But one way or another, I am certain our mutual friend is the one who intends to receive his message — and when the exchange is made, you must be watching."

———————

THE BOY'S NAME WAS Peter Moon. He was Eileen's age. Likely younger. A Carolina artilleryman who'd lost a right arm and suffered ragged burns and gashes to the left before he was captured.

More had to be sacrificed.

"Gangrene," snorted Madeleine Coffin as she charged through the hospital grounds. "In the left arm. He hid it from us, the poor idiot. If we'd caught it sooner, maybe we could have saved the arm, but now..."

She shook her head and waved for Eileen to trot faster. Soon they were both in the amputation tent, holding Peter Moon to the bloody-brown table while the surgeon went to work. Eileen gave him a snort of whiskey but he vomited it back out as soon as the bone saw appeared. She dropped the bottle onto the grass. Ms. Coffin scolded her and gently caressed Peter Moon's cheek while she put a wooden spoon in his teeth.

The surgeon took little notice of the two women. Or the boy, really. The three of them were nothing but specters while he sliced through skin and muscle until he hit bone. The blade must have struck an artery because a thin column of blood shot out of the wound and struck Ms. Coffin's waist.

"You crimp that nice and tight, girl," she barked without a hint of squeamishness.

Eileen screwed the tourniquet wrapped around the boy's arm tighter and tighter. The surgeon dropped one tool and picked up a second. Then came the awful sounds of the bone saw's iron teeth working its way through the bone, and Peter Moon's horrible, muffled wails.

The limb came off and the surgeon shoved Eileen to the side so he could seal the wound. Ms. Coffin wrapped the lifeless arm in linens and pulled Eileen out of the tent, their shoes squelching through congealed blood in the grass.

The amputation took less than a minute. Peter Moon died half an hour later.

Ms. Coffin was the only woman Eileen had ever known to smoke a pipe.

They sat together on a log pile and watched the gravediggers shovel out a new hole for Peter Moon. The previous night's rain was long gone. Giant snowflakes drifted about them, doomed to melt away on the soggy ground.

Ms. Coffin lit a plug of her bitter-smelling tobacco. Eileen watched the shovels. Peter Moon's arm lay between them, bleeding through its linen wrappings.

"Should've told us about the gangrene," grunted Ms. Coffin. "Didn't want us to cut off the arm, did he? Well, now look where that's got him."

Eileen slowly turned her gaze to take in Ms. Coffin's profile. She was unmarried but hardly an old maid. The streaks of silver in her brown hair were painted by stress more than age—similar, in fact, to Ms. Charlotte's own silvering hair.

The Coffin sisters were from one of those great Columbus families, first settlers on the banks of the Scioto River back when George Washington was President. Socially, Eileen and Ms. Coffin were just about as far apart as one could imagine. But here they both were, tending to thousands of sick, wounded, wretched rebel prisoners.

Ms. Coffin finished her smoke and plucked the pipe from her teeth. Then she opened the small purse lashed to her belt. Every time they lost a patient, Ms. Coffin rummaged through her little purse and plucked out two Indian head pennies to place over their eyes just before burial.

"For the ferryman," she always said.

This time Ms. Coffin retrieved four pennies. Eileen took notice. As far as she knew, only Peter Moon had expired that day.

"Who else has died?"

Ms. Coffin stared at the treetops on the horizon and idly jingled the pennies in her hand. "The officer from the First Alabama. Lieutenant Creighton. This morning, before you arrived. Haven't buried him yet, of course. Wouldn't want to send him across the river without fare."

Eileen shuddered. "What happened?"

"Nerves, maybe," said Ms. Coffin. "A condition of the heart. Perhaps a weak constitution. Can't spend too much time thinking about it, now can we?"

Ms. Coffin spat out a glob of tobacco-stained saliva and jingled her pennies.

THEY'D PUT PENNIES OVER her mother's eyes, too. She'd come all the way across the ocean. She trusted the promise of America. She died in Columbus, Ohio a year later.

They had buried her at the North Graveyard with a simple stone bearing her name, facing the East, anticipating Jesus Christ's glorious return. For the moment, though, she faced only towers of black smoke spewing from the train depot across High Street.

Eileen was sitting quietly on a nearby tombstone staring at her mother's grave when the snow started to come down thick and swift. She heard a great rustling as someone wearing a noisy, frilled dress sat on another stone behind her.

"You signaled," said Ms. Charlotte.

"Robert Creighton is dead," Eileen answered.

There was an uncomfortable shuffling of fabric behind her. From the corner of her eye and through the snow, Eileen spotted the black coach and its four angry horses waiting at the cemetery gate.

"It makes perfect sense," said Ms. Charlotte. "She received her message and disposed of the young lieutenant as soon as he was no longer useful to her."

"I just don't know that she would do such a thing."

"I know what you're thinking, young lady," snapped the woman. "You think that because she's the only person in this city who seems to care about the poor, pathetic rebels, she would never murder one of them? Of course she would. She would, because she is a traitor. Because she is a spy." Ms. Charlotte sighed. There was more uncomfortable rustling. "I did not want a direct confrontation, but it appears necessary."

"Perhaps you should go to the authorities?" Eileen suggested.

"I would not be listened to," said Ms. Charlotte. "She has charmed everyone. It must be proven bluntly, or it will not be proven at all. And you shall help me."

Eileen's face blanched. "Me?"

"I cannot trust anyone else," said Ms. Charlotte. "It will be an easy task. No danger at all. It is not my first choice, mind you, but no danger at all. And a bonus atop what I've already paid you. Yes, it must be you."

THAT NIGHT, THE SERVANTS ushered Eileen into the Coffin House through their entrance. She hid herself in the empty parlor, listening to the help prepare for dinner in other rooms of the mansion. The room felt as though it had gone unused for many years, the furniture hidden by sheets and the fireplace lonely and cold. The floor was covered with a thin layer of dust and ancient cigar ash.

She hid in a corner between the great window and the door. She nearly jumped when a shadow swept across the frosted glass. Just before eight o'clock, she heard a knock at the great door to the foyer.

A servant opened the door. "Ah, Ms. Coffin. It's lovely to see you back here again."

"Thank you," Ms. Madeleine Coffin replied. "I was surprised to be summoned, indeed, but happy to be home. Is my sister about?"

Eileen heard new footsteps in the foyer, followed by her employer's voice. "Madeleine! Right on time as always."

Eileen peeked through the sliver of space between the parlor door and its frame. She saw her employer step past her servant and kiss Ms. Coffin on both cheeks.

"Charlotte," said Ms. Coffin. "It's been a long time."

"I know, it has," said Charlotte Coffin. "But it's Christmas, after all, and I know Father would have wanted us to celebrate together. Come along inside and shut out the cold. Thomas shall take your bag to the guest room. You will say for the holiday, won't you?"

Eileen watched the two sisters disappear from the foyer while Thomas the servant climbed the great staircase with a carpet valise in hand.

When she was confident they'd all left, she pushed the door open and crept into the foyer. A gasolier lit her way as she stepped closer to the dining room door. She compelled her heart to beat slower so she might hear the Coffin sisters.

"It's a remarkable change," said Madeleine. "Haven't seen the place in such good condition. It must have been quite a lot of work."

"Indeed," said Charlotte. "And there is still a long way to go, I'm afraid — ah, thank you."

Eileen heard plates being set on the table as the help began to serve dinner.

"The parlor still needs to be renovated, and the wine cellar," said Charlotte. "But soon I think I shall have this place back up to the proper North End standards. It's what Father would have wanted."

Madeleine Coffin chuckled. "Father would have wanted us plump, married and lazy, not irritable spinsters working ourselves to the bone."

"Yes, well, you always had such a low opinion of Father."

"Not without reason," said Madeleine. "He did allow this place to fall into disrepair."

"Come now—"

"And I am sure you have exhausted much of your inheritance getting it back up to snuff," said Madeleine. "Am I wrong, little sister? He was a good man, yes — but he might have seen to his finances before his philanthropy."

"I am surprised to find you so critical of charity," said Charlotte. "Given your efforts on behalf of the rebel prisoners."

"Charity is a virtue," said Madeleine. "But draining our family resources on his abolitionist crusade — especially considering this ghastly war it's dragged the country into — well, perhaps it's more prudent to devote one's attention to affairs of the home."

"I see," said Charlotte.

"I do not mean to insult you, sister," said Madeleine. "As I said, you've done such fine work getting it all back in order. But Father's eccentricities — and that inexplicable obsession with abolition — it was always a bit much."

Eileen crept away from the dining room door and back into the foyer. She climbed the stairs as nimbly as she could and made straight for the guest room.

She inserted Ms. Charlotte's key into the door, twisted, and stepped inside. Ms. Coffin's carpet valise sat on the bed. The room was dark but for the streetlights flickering through the snow in the windows. Eileen wasted no time.

She did not know what she was looking for in the valise, only that Ms. Charlotte was certain her sister would be carrying a secret message from the rebel officer Robert Creighton. Eileen had doubts, and those doubts increased as she discovered nothing but spare clothing in Ms. Coffin's bag.

Perhaps this will be the end of it, thought Eileen as she closed the bag and backed away from the bed. She would tell Ms. Charlotte there was nothing to incriminate Madeleine Coffin, and if she wanted to keep on believing her sister was a traitor, she could do so. But Eileen would be finished with the whole business.

Just then, the girl gazed out through the snow and caught sight of the coach in the alley. The four angry horses had been led away to the stable, but Ms. Charlotte's black coach sat idle as snow piled atop its roof. Then Eileen recalled that Ms. Charlotte had dispatched the coach to retrieve Ms. Madeleine and carry her back to the Coffin House.

Madeleine Coffin might be just as suspicious as her sister, thought Eileen. If she suspected what was on her sister's mind, she might have also suspected her belongings would be searched.

When she returned to the bottom of the stairs, Eileen could tell by the tone and volume of the sisters' muffled voices that the conversation in the dining room had become heated. She quickly walked away from the dining room door and down the foyer, quietly slipping out the front door and into the snow.

Tugging her shawl tight around her body, she crunched through the snow and around the house to the alley. Somehow, without the four angry horses, the black coach seemed less daunting and dreadful. Eileen pulled herself up off the snow and swung open the door.

She saw nothing inside. Nothing on the seats and nothing on the floor. It had been a foolish misadventure. Why should a spy — if indeed Ms. Coffin was a spy — hide a secret message here? To retrieve later, perhaps. But why carry it with her to the Coffin House at all?

Eileen shivered. Ms. Charlotte's obsession about her sister was dangerously close to becoming her own. She desperately wanted to give her employer something to justify her pay, some intelligence that simply wasn't there. She shifted her body across the leather seat, back towards the door of the coach. That is when she felt it.

It was stuffed between the seat cushions. Eileen reached her hand into the crease and pulled out Ms. Coffin's purse. It was heavy and it jingled. She loosened the purse's drawstrings and peered inside. Atop a pile of Indian head pennies sat a folded square of paper.

Her heart beat faster. She opened the paper and held it close to the window, trying to catch what little light she could from the nearest streetlamp.

My dearest Madeleine,

How terrible that we should have found each other on the eve of this horrible war, and that by no choice of our own we should find ourselves on opposing sides. There was a time not long ago when I would have proudly fought and died for the South and all her enduring glory. But now I think only of you. I care nothing for returning home if it means I must spend another hour away from you. In a day or so, I shall surrender to the Federals. If they will take me alive, I shall use whatever finesse I can muster to get myself sent to Columbus. If I do not survive, however, I can only hope this letter finds its way to you. In either case, know that I shall spend the rest of my days madly in love with you, and you alone.

I shall see you again, my love — in Columbus or in Heaven.

Sincerely,
Robert Creighton

Eileen had barely read the letter before she heard a commotion at the front of the Coffin House. When she trudged out from the alley clutching Madeleine's heavy purse, she saw Thomas holding open the front door, ushering out the other servants.

"What's happened?" said Eileen.

"They've commenced to fightin' in there," said Thomas. "You'd best stay out of it."

He left the front door and guided the others through the snow. She knew not where they would go, but presumably it was a less chaotic place.

Eileen marched through the foyer to the dining room. She could hear the Coffin sisters shouting. When she opened the door, neither of the sisters turned her way. There was nothing else in the world to them, nothing but their hatred for each other.

Madeleine Coffin stood with her back to Eileen on one side of a table decorated with an uneaten Christmas feast. Charlotte Coffin stood on the other side of the table, her back to an old roll top writing desk set against the wall. The room was red and orange with hot, glowing candlelight.

"How dare you think yourself worthy of criticizing our father?" Charlotte screamed. "You who abandoned us! You who abandoned your own country!"

"I'll not hear any more insinuations about my loyalty," snapped Madeleine. "I know you have been slandering me all over this city, and I have always turned the other cheek. But now I am at my wit's end, Charlotte — it is time to put aside childish things!"

"Childish!?"

"Your petulant hatred of me was barely tolerable when we were children, but now we are grown!" screamed Madeleine. "We are real women and this is a real war and you cannot go around making up your little stories about me any longer!"

"I have never made up anything!" Charlotte shouted back. "I have always seen through you, ever since we were children! You charm everyone else, but I always knew! You lie and you manipulate, and you are exactly the kind of duplicitous coward the filthy rebels would have spying for them—"

By this time, Madeleine Coffin had walked around the table to deliver a severe smack across her little sister's face. Charlotte stumbled from the blow and in doing so knocked a candle from the table.

"Oh, dear, Charlotte," gasped Madeleine. "I am sorry. Please, let me help you—"

But then there was a soft burst of orange light and both sisters saw that the fallen candle had ignited the leg of the rolltop desk.

"No!" screamed Charlotte. "Father's desk!"

"Leave it, Charlotte," said Madeleine. "We must snuff it out!"

But Charlotte Coffin paid no mind to snuffing out the fire. She slid open the desk and began flinging papers and envelopes and other trinkets out of it, trying to save them from the growing flames.

"Charlotte, we must leave!" said Madeleine as she stepped away from the desk and back around to her side of the table.

"This was all Father's!" sobbed Charlotte.

"This is madness, Charlotte," said Madeleine. "Are you having another of your episodes?"

"This was his!" shrieked Charlotte as she took a small folding knife from the desk and tossed it onto the table.

"And this was his!"

A pocket watch clattered across the table and slipped onto the floor.

"And this was his, too."

When she turned around, Charlotte Coffin had tears streaming down her cheeks and an Army revolver in both of her hands. The fire engulfed the desk and melted the wallpaper and silhouetted Charlotte as she trained the gun on her sister's chest.

"Charlotte…" murmured Madeleine as she slowly raised her hands.

"Stop it!" screamed Eileen from the doorway. "Stop it, Ms. Coffin, put that gun down!"

Somehow that was the first moment when the Coffin sisters noticed Eileen. Madeleine's face betrayed a mix of shock and anger, realizing that for some strange reason the young Irish camp nurse was in her family home.

"You?" said Madeleine. "What are you doing here?"

Eileen ignored her and stared at her employer. "This is wrong, Ms. Charlotte. You are wrong."

"What?" said Ms. Charlotte.

Eileen held up the letter in one hand and the purse in the other. "You've been wrong the whole time. Your sister isn't a traitor, she isn't a spy. Neither was Robert Creighton. They loved each other. That was the message he brought. That is why he wanted to be sent to Camp Chase. And now she suffers and mourns for him. Can't you find any sympathy for her? Are you so blinded by your hatred?"

The gun trembled in Charlotte's hands and her legs seemed to wobble. Her eyes grew desperately wide as she glanced between her sister and Eileen. The fire behind her easily spread to the wall and flew up to the ceiling.

"Please drop the gun," begged Eileen. "This house is going to burn. If we don't get out, we're all going to die—"

But as soon as Eileen stepped close enough, Madeleine Coffin struck the girl across the face, much as she struck Charlotte. And, much like Charlotte, Eileen stumbled from the blow and the letter from Robert Creighton fluttered out of her hand and onto the table.

Madeleine didn't seem to notice or care. Instead, she yanked the purse from Eileen's hand, spilling a shower of Indian head pennies onto the floor.

Whether purposefully or not, Charlotte fired her revolver. A plate on the table exploded. Eileen dropped to the floor and shrieked. Above her, Madeleine pulled a derringer from its hiding place under the pennies and aimed it at Charlotte.

They both fired at the same time. They both fell at the same time.

Madeleine Coffin's body collapsed with a thud next to Eileen. The girl saw a dark, scarlet hole just above the woman's right, lifeless eye. On the other side of the table, Charlotte Coffin groaned.

Eileen rushed around the table and pulled her employer away from the oppressive heat of the ravenous fire. She dragged the woman back around the table and propped her up against the doorway. It was a stomach wound, and Eileen knew it was unsurvivable. She had seen plenty like it.

"Keep your hands on it, just like this," she said. "Keep pressure on the wound, don't let it bleed. I'll get you outside and the fire brigade will come shortly."

But Ms. Charlotte would only shake her head and smile. "I was right…" she mumbled in a shaking voice. "I was right…"

Eileen looked down at the woman's hands. They were not putting pressure on the wound as instructed. They were clutching the letter that slipped from Eileen's hands and fluttered across the table. She must have snatched it just before the shooting started.

Eileen took the letter from her. On one side was the message from the doomed and lovestruck Lieutenant Robert Creighton. On the other side, faint writing appeared with every new wave of heat wafting from the dining room inferno.

Lines of numbers and letters. A code written in invisible ink. Eileen stared wide-eyed at Madeleine Coffin's crumpled body.

"I was right," mumbled Charlotte as life finally drifted out of her. "I was right."

—THE END—

About the Author

Jesse Bethea is an award-winning journalist and author living in Columbus, Ohio with his wife and three cats. His short fiction has appeared in a number of magazines and anthologies in the United States and abroad. His first novel, *Fellow Travellers,* was published in 2021.

The Tips of One's Fingers

By Lance Mason

Notable Advances in Criminal Detection as gathered from documents provided from the private papers of those described herein; footnotes added for clarity.

By Lt. Col. Hugh Christopher Gough-Martin, FRCS (LON), MB ChB (Edin)

Preface

ON 6 NOVEMBER 1892, a tea-chest of documents, diaries, and other historical material was found in Bombay, languishing in the dusty corner of a warehouse belonging to Marlowe & Sons, a prominent Liverpool shipping firm engaged in the India trade. It was eventually established that this battered and misplaced container was the property of my father, Brig. Gen. Jonathan "Jock" Alexander Gough-Martin, IOM, DSO, and had been lost during his return to Britain with his regiment nearly four years previous.

Once Father was identified as the rightful owner, we were traced through military records and our Lancashire relations, and the large, tin-lined box was shipped to us via Suez, Gibraltar, and Southampton, arriving mid-March 1893. Sadly, Jock died shortly thereafter, aged sixty-eight years.

It has taken the better part of three years to organize Father's papers, and read, interpret, and research them. Meanwhile, I've communicated with well-informed persons, verified claims, and transcribed what follows.

I caution that not all of the following was chronicled in, or drawn from, the chest's papers. Of that which Father did not have first-hand knowledge, I am most grateful for the access provided me to the private diaries, journals, records, and vivid memories of other persons, some of renown and featured here, some readers will recognize, and others who laboured nobly but in obscurity.

I have put this account in the form of a story, in order that the reader might be entertained as well as informed.

Due to poetic license being used to bridge minor gaps in these pages, some readers may cite errors or disputes with this record, and raise debate where they find it lacking. It is not my place to contest these assertions, but to put forth the reality of what I have before me and let history judge its merits.

14 January 1896
Hugh Christopher Gough-Martin,
FRCS (Edin), MB ChB
Field Cottage
Godalming, Surrey

Author's Note

The use herein of a medical viewpoint was much aided by my friend and colleague Peter Turnbull, appointed Surgeon-General, Government of Bombay in 1893.

In addition, as a schoolboy, I knew J. Arjani, and a more upright and ethical person one couldn't expect to meet. It was he who inspired me to take up medicine, much to the pleasure of my father.

2 March 1896
H.C. Gough-Martin

Publishers Note

The reader will note many years' span between the author's dates above and publication of this volume. Due to potentially upsetting passages contained herein, and not heretofore revealed regarding the life of Florence Nightingale, OM RRC LGStJ, the publishers felt it necessary to defer the book's release until after her death, which has now, to our great regret, come to pass.

This is meant to honour her venerable and respected reputation as one of the Empire's leading lights, and in consideration of her family and the causes for which Miss Nightingale dedicated her life.

Gareth Morgan, Editor
Greenwich Meridian Books
Greenwich, London

Part I — Arjani and Friends

On a Friday in late September 1883, St. Bartholomew's Hospital hosted a dinner in The Great Hall to honor the renowned medical scientist Sir James Paget, celebrating his elevation to Vice Chancellor of the University of London. His close friend Florence Nightingale and her paramour Professor Arjani attended as Paget's special guests and, following the meal and speeches of well-deserved praise, Sir James sat with them for a friendly chat over glasses of port.[1]

"I was pleased to see you two at the table this evening," he said. "One doesn't see one's friends nearly as much as one should. What news do you have for me, if any?"

Nightingale smiled and nodded at her companion, Jehangir Arjani. Paget had introduced them years ago, well before his own professorship, having described Barts' new surgeon to Florence as having formerly served with Her Majesty's forces in The East — India, Persia, and Crimea — the latter being the theatre of war in which Nightingale first garnered her renown.

Arjani began. "Well, Sir James, while in the dissection theatre today with the senior Anatomy students, I saw two familiar faces at the back of the group. When my lecture was finished, I invited them into the Anatomy Library to ask the cause of their visit. You recall John Watson and Sherlock Holmes?"

Paget's expression said he did. "Watson the Scotsman? Yes, took his degree here and was later wounded overseas. And Holmes — rather eccentric, as I recall, whom no one actually knew. Part-time researcher at Barts, though cold as a fish, some said."

"Correct on all counts, Sir James," Arjani said, "other than some debate on John's place of birth."

Nightingale spoke. "Jehan and I developed an attachment to John as a student in his final year at Barts."

---

1. From humble beginnings, and now risen to be a preeminent *persona medicini* of our age, Sir James Paget is a prolific, proficient researcher and medical mind, who has elevated our expectations of ourselves in the medical profession in more ways than we can count.

Nodding, Paget asked, "And what can you tell us, Professor, about the current version of Watson and Holmes?"

"The two seem to have formed an odd collaboration," Arjani said. "Difficult to define, exactly. Watson, in a certain way, seems to keep Holmes on the straight and narrow. Helps him refine his thoughts — when Holmes hasn't disappeared."

Paget sipped his port. "Disappeared? Does he travel a good deal?"

"No, Sir James," said Arjani. "Disappear — as in vanish from sight."

Nightingale chortled. "Jehan, please."

Paget smiled, but added a squint. "So, he's a phantom, a ghost, as well as eccentric?"

"We haven't got to the bottom of it with Watson," Arjani replied. "He only tells us that he occasionally loses sight of Holmes within the flat, with all doors and windows closed. He says the man has occasionally disappeared on the street."

"But eventually returns, one assumes?" Paget took another drink.

"Yes, always," said Nightingale, "but otherwise won't discuss the thing with Watson. Calls it part of his 'endeavours as a consulting detective.'"

"And what does he mean by that?" Paget asked.

Arjani nodded. "My question, as well. Presumably, someone with training and experience in a specific field. Much as we in medicine would refer to you, Sir James, as a Consultant Pathologist, or me as a Consultant Surgeon. Perhaps Holmes adopted it when he worked in the labs here, believing it confers a certain authenticity or expertise to his work."

"Which is what?" asked Sir James.

"Some assisting in police investigations," Arjani said, "some in wholly private matters." A secret glance between him and Nightingale recalled the sounds and smells of a violent death a decade before in Bedford Court, Covent Garden, an event about which neither ever spoke, except to each other. "It seems Holmes has an ability to absorb factual evidence — what he stubbornly calls data, plural of datum — that others seem to find unintelligible."

"And what, may I ask," Sir James remarked with a grin, "was he detecting in your anatomy lecture? Something nefarious, no doubt."

"Exactly my concern," Arjani said, also smiling. "It seems he has a practical interest in the unique patterns on the skin on individuals' fingers and hands. He argues that, being distinct in each person, these can be used to distinguish individuals."

Paget, spectacles in place, was now examining his own fingertips.

Arjani continued. "He believes that a method to record them can serve to investigate the perpetrators of crimes. To illuminate the discussion, I produced my collection of magnifying glasses, a present from my Uncle Zubin on my departure from India. Holmes was captivated by their usefulness."

"But surely," Nightingale said, "such lenses are nothing new. Evolved in the 13th Century, I believe, when Bacon invented them."

"True," Arjani said, "but neither Holmes nor Watson wear spectacles, at least not yet. So, neither has the daily benefit of artificial optics, as it were. Despite Holmes's proficiency with a microscope, the practical advantage of a hand-held glass had just not yet struck him. Now he is elated. A devoted convert."

"And you believe there is some value in these..." Paget asked, "...these skin patterns?"

"Without question," Arjani replied. "They've been recognized in India for centuries, as identification in business contracts. A man Herschel used them in Bengal 30, 40 years ago. And Henry, a British policeman, also in Bengal, uses them today in his criminal investigation work. Rumors say they are used in China, also."

"So, as usual," Paget said, "the British have fallen behind." The three of them recognized some truth in the great man's jest. "Yet I hear a chap 'round London, name of Galton, a relation of Darwin, has been collecting data — Holmes's term for it — on these finger-marks."[2]

Yes," said Arjani, "Holmes has been collecting references on these things, and they have piqued his interest."

Bemused, Nightingale said, "And did Holmes give any indication of his current need for this so-called data? Or should I ask?"

"A private affair," said Arjani. "Talk of a theft, it seems, one of considerable value. A prominent family's heirloom jewelry, and our 'consulting detective' has been consulted."

Nightingale scoffed. "But the police have not?"

---

2. Francis Galton's published work in this field has not yet been fully tested for applicable utility. As a result, the Metropolitan Police have not adopted it, despite Holmes' growing conviction of the methodology's value.

"A concern," Arjani said, "that a member of this family, one from the higher classes, could be implicated in the crime. Even our friend Watson hasn't been given the name."

"Such melodrama," Paget said, and then turned to Nightingale. "You know Watson well, m'lady?" He used the term from respect, not as a title.

"Jehan and I socialized freely with him around Barts," she said, "before his training at Netley Hospital, in Hampshire. From Netley, it was off to the Northwest frontier and the war there. His only war."

Arjani shook his head. "I encouraged his career interest in India and sometimes feel responsible for his injury."

"Now, now," Paget said, "all those who influence soldiers can't be blamed for their wounds."

"Otherwise," Nightingale said, "our entire nation would be wallowing in guilt."

Paget smiled. "From one who knows far more than most on the subject. In fact, Florence, you were of great assistance to the Queen, were you not, in bringing Netley into existence?"

"Alas, by the time Her Majesty requested my views on matters, it was a juggernaut. Still, great work has been done there for our soldiers."

Paget then turned a wry smile to Arjani. "Tell us more about these Indian finger marks."

"That about sums it up, for now. I told Holmes he was on the right track, that identifying individuals by such patterns was certainly a legitimate technique, and that the great fund of anatomical knowledge here at St. Bartholomew's was at his disposal in bringing justice to the Empire's criminals."

Paget's grin enlarged. "Pray this won't lead to the execution of any of us."

Part II — Arjani, Jewels, and Obstacles to Justice

A native of Poona, India, a Parsi, and a Zoroastrian, Jehangir Arjani, now Professor of Anatomy and Surgery at St. Bartholomew's Hospital (founded 1123), had served in the 1853-56 Crimean War, a Russo-British conflict. Following the Battle of Mamelon, Arjani had been captured and forced to attend the Russian wounded in field hospitals under the pioneering and highly regarded Muscovite surgeon Nikolai Pirogov. Remarkably, after many useful lessons at Pirogov's side, Arjani escaped due to the indefatigable bravery of a fellow prisoner, Sergeant Major Dominic Cartwright of the 4th Dragoon Guards. He rescued Arjani on a dark summer night by stealing the horse of a Cossack Lancer and galloping both he and Arjani back to British lines under a hail of Russian musket fire.

After Crimea, returning by ship with the British Army to India, and on exiting the Gulf of Aden, Arjani was sidetracked to the brief but fierce Anglo-Persian War, 1856-1857. In the wake of that victory, his comrade and dearest friend, Major Angus Stirling, was murdered late at night in a Muscat *souk*. Yet prior to this, and unknown to Arjani, Stirling had been secretly — and very romantically — involved with Florence Nightingale in Crimea and had often spoken fondly to her of Arjani. Thus, several years later in London, Nightingale recognized Paget's description of Barts' "new surgeon, a Parsi gentleman, battlefield experience with Her Majesty's forces in Crimea."

It was well after these facts, of course, that Nightingale and Arjani's acquaintance became something more than professional.

WITHIN A FEW DAYS of mentioning the unsolved jewelry theft to James Paget, the time had arrived for Jehan Arjani to have another meeting with Holmes and Watson, the first since the Anatomy Library. They seated themselves in Arjani's study at Barts.

"Mr. Holmes, I hope you'll indulge me," Arjani said. "How goes your case of the unnamed family's stolen heirlooms?"

"I'm honored, Doctor Arjani," Holmes said, "that you wish to hear my disquisition on this case."

"I'd be grateful for your time, sir," Arjani replied, "and intrigued to hear your logical application of any information you've gathered."

"Any data, you mean," Holmes said.

"Precisely," Arjani said.

"If you can be patient," Holmes replied, "I will lay out the entire story, or as much as I know. I see you have a notebook and pencil. Please don't interrupt. Just make notes of any questions you have, and I'll address them once I've concluded."

Arjani was not the least surprised by Holmes's dictation of terms, which fit his *modus operandi*. "At your convenience, sir."

Holmes began. "As I explained previously, a quantity of heirloom jewelry went missing from a collection in the well-appointed residence of a moneyed family off Grosvenor Square,

Mayfair. The parents have long since passed on, and the house is shared by two sisters and a brother, whom I'll call Mandrake. Mandrake claims to have discovered the loss of this treasure when he entered one of the upstairs dressing rooms and found, on the floor, the velvet-and-satin-lined walnut chest in which the missing items, the cache of jewels, had been held. Because the older sister, whom I'll call Rowena, was a known drinker, gambler, and spendthrift, Mandrake had to consider if she had been guilty of the theft.

"Through well-connected friends, Mandrake called on me to search for any clues that might exonerate or implicate Rowena, if not prove her guilt outright. Clearly, a sensitive and awkward situation. As a matter of course, on payment of my retainer, I asked Mandrake if these possessions were insured. He said they were, which posed another consideration second to the identity of the perpetrator. That is, if Lloyd's, the insurer, paid on the loss, and Rowena herself was the undiscovered thief, then she would get her share of Lloyd's payment plus whatever other funds she raised from the illicit sale of the stolen goods."

During all of Holmes's account, Arjani noticed that Watson sat unmoving — not rigid, but quite still — seeming to focus on nothing but Holmes's eyes and words.

"However," Holmes said, "back to the facts. After my thorough inspection of the scene, it was evident that it was a domestic crime." Arjani looked bemused. Holmes translated. "That is, a crime committed within the domestic confines of a home or other property by a resident of that property. A family member, per se, is not necessarily guilty. Perhaps a servant, but not someone dwelling outside the said property.

"I'd estimate that a man of your stature in medicine, Dr. Arjani — or should I say Mr. Arjani — is never bored by cogent details, and I will provide them.[3]

"I searched the dressing room in which Mandrake claimed to have found the empty jewelry chest, as well as a second upstairs dressing room, the surrounding hall, landings, staircases, downstairs foyer, and possible ground- and first-floor entries — the sources of data one would expect." Holmes continued ticking items off his mental list. "I further searched the living quarters of the three siblings, those of the live-in staff, as well as the storage rooms, pantries, kitchen, and the basement and its access."

Logic told Arjani that Watson had already been apprised of these findings, and so enquired for himself. "May I conclude, by your describing this as a 'domestic crime,' that you found no evidence of foreign entry, forced or otherwise?"

"Correct. None on or around any external portals, doors, or windows," Holmes said, "nor in the approaches to them. In addition, neither the dressing room door nor the chest had been forced. Therefore, yes, the conclusion is of a domestic crime."

"And the staff?" asked Arjani. "Any of them under suspicion."

Watson shook his head but spoke only after eye contact with Holmes. "The chambermaid's brother spent three months in the nick a few years back, but he is aboard ship now, doing the

---

3. Though not always recognized, it is the custom in British medicine to address surgeons as "Mr." rather than "Dr." As with dentists, this derives from their origins as barbers.

sugar and tobacco runs from Jamaica. She's been with the family more than three years, clean as a whistle. Same with the others."

Holmes said, "The staff have keys to the dressing rooms, but not to the jewelry chest, which was indeed opened by means of a key. No evidence of force."

"And after your search," Arjani said, "the three siblings have provided no further clues, no direction for your investigation?"

"I did not immediately divulge my definitive findings to Mandrake," Holmes said. "I decided to cogitate on them a bit, so they are not yet aware of my deductions. However, about the time I first discussed this case with you, I did insist Mandrake report the loss to Lloyd's. Then, before noon on the Friday just gone, he terminated my consultancy, which seemed to end any suspicions he had of Rowena being guilty in the theft."

"And you've had no cause," Arjani asked, "to pursue the use of finger-marks?"

"It seems not," Holmes said.

"No suspicious fingers," Watson said, somewhat bitterly, "hence no suspicious marks."

THE FIRST DISCUSSION WITH Arjani in the Anatomy Library, combined with the second meeting in Arjani's study, gave Holmes and Watson cause to return intermittently to Arjani for guidance, debate, or confirmation — at times, all three — on several other matters to do with Holmes's detective work, public and private. In turn, Arjani found gratification in the friendly but logical jousting with them over data, deduction, and Holmes's occasionally eccentric conclusions in regard to the cases. He had yet to "see" Holmes disappear and had not raised the point again with Watson.

Many weeks after Sir James Paget's celebration dinner at Barts' Great Hall, on a frigid night in early December, with London cloaked in fog and choking on coal smoke, the three men found seats near the fire in the Jugged Hare on Chiswell Street in Finsbury. Wearing a grim look, Watson returned from the bar with three fragrant mugs of wassail.[4]

"Our regrets, Professor," he said, "at being long away from your company. Holmes and I have been working with Special Branch on these Irish maniacs who've been bombing the Underground. Little headway, I'm afraid."

"Yes, the work of monsters," said Arjani. "We've seen many of the injuries in Barts' wards. And what of your work? Have you gentlemen any news on the missing jewels of Mayfair?"

Holmes expression conveyed some portent. "Weeks after we last spoke, a note arrived for me from Lloyd's, where I have long-standing ties. They wished me to come 'round and advise them on an as-yet unspoken matter."

Watson glanced at Holmes before slipping his pipestem from his teeth. He spoke as if from a script. "As the Metropolitan Police at Scotland Yard learn more of criminal detection, and of the investigation of the scenes and perpetrators of crimes, Lloyd's and similar firms have begun requiring a detailed police report to verify alleged thefts."

---

4. A cider mulled with cloves and cinnamon.

Holmes took over. "My collaborator at Lloyd's confirmed Mandrake had indeed begun a claim, and was told that, before reimbursement for any claimed loss, Lloyd's would require such a police report. It was at that point that, as I told you weeks ago, Mandrake immediately cancelled his arrangement with me to look into any ties between Rowena and the theft.

"With Mandrake's nod, the police began their investigation by taking away the walnut jewel case as evidence, along with two lesser jewelry pieces not stolen. I was asked by Scotland Yard to remove these items for detailed inspection at the flat I share with Watson, and was assured, particularly by Inspector Lestrade, that this was without Mandrake's knowledge. Since then, as per our discussion, I have been detecting and recording a great many finger-marks left on the box, dusting it with a white powder of my own formulation, then transferring the results onto sheets of black paper coated thinly with adhesive. Most of my time is spent obtaining the various images, discriminating between them, and grouping them into matching sets, where your recent gift of a fine-quality hand lens has been a great aid to the labour."

"Gratifying," said Arjani, with growing excitement, "very gratifying. And what have you found?"

Watson said, cautiously, what Holmes seemed to avoid. "Too soon to know. A great deal more work to do. Quite painstaking, requiring great precision. Solitary stuff. Holmes seems the perfect man for it, I'd say." The two men exchanged looks Arjani couldn't interpret.

"I have interviewed the police themselves," Holmes said. "How many had handled the box? Fortuitously, only one, Inspector Noyce's man Hollings, whom I believe you know."

"Yes," Arjani said, "from the Covent Garden shooting some years back. The deceased had murdered a number of British soldiers in the regions of India. Someone got their revenge here in London against that killer and made a clean escape. Despite my knowledge of the India murders, I wasn't able to help the police on the local shooting."

"Yes, well, Asst. Insp. Hollings's marks were on the box," Watson said, a bit informally, Arjani noticed, "but he had an ironclad alibi for the night of the theft. In Blackheath, an England-Wales rugby football fixture. A dozen witnesses."

Holmes added, "So that left two suspects' finger-marks, three at most, to identify."

"Mandrake," Arjani said, "Rowena, and the second sister? And you believe Mandrake no longer suspects Rowena?"

Holmes drummed his third finger against the tabletop. "No indication. However, with your opinion, my guidance, and Lloyd's encouragement, the police have requested the presence at Whitehall Lane of the three siblings to have their finger patterns taken and recorded so they could be eliminated as Sergeant Hollings has been."

"And when should that be?" Arjani wanted to know.

"Yesterday," Watson said, "if Holmes had his way. But, with luck, before Christmas."

Before speaking, Holmes gave Watson a look that seemed to douse his enthusiasm. "It is my conviction that there will be a great deal to come from the study of finger-marks, but Lestrade and the others at the Yard continue to resist. It is for that reason that they put the items in my hands, but I see it as a Sisyphus-like struggle to sway them."

Watson exhaled, deadpan. "Science seems to mean nothing to them."

After seeing Arjani into a Hansom cab for the return back to his flat, Holmes and Watson ducked back into the pub.

Holmes began refilling his pipe. "Tell me more, Watson, about your ties to the good professor and Miss Nightingale."

As usual, Watson found himself cautious at providing personal details to Holmes. On all things practical, his trust in Holmes was like steel, though Holmes consistently showed a greater grasp in that world than Watson. On the intangibles, however, in the world of internal matters, Watson found Holmes to be nearly bereft of the feelings and sensitivities a man occasionally longs to share. However, at this question, which took him back to his youth before Holmes, Watson seemed to shake off any hesitancy.

"During my degree year at Barts, Mr. Arjani was goaded by an arrogant student in Surgery Lab into discussing an article in *The Lancet* on the work of Nikolai Pirogov, the peerless Russian battlefield surgeon. Unbeknownst to any of us, Arjani was not only well-versed on the methods, but, as a prisoner of the Russians in Crimea, had actually worked in surgical theatre with Pirogov, a matter he had never boasted about. However, as the hooligan student antagonized him, he began to reveal to us his history in combat, and the entire body of us were captivated, swept away in a sort of delirium, to be in the company of a man who had actually lived the sort of tales that Tennyson and others had made immortal.[5]

"When I later expressed my own interest in both India and the Army, Mr. Arjani was most generous with his time. He and Miss Nightingale invited me to dine, and even to the theatre. He inspired me, then I was taken on at Netley, and, before I knew it, I was overseas. You know the rest — the 2nd Afghan War, the disaster at Maiwand."

"What do you know," asked Holmes, "about these murders that he mentioned, his work with Noyce and Hollings on this business in Covent Garden?"

Watson drew a long sigh. "Going back many years, long before the professor's time in London, there had been a string of murders of British soldiers in India, Burma, and even Muscat, where Mr. Arjani lost an army comrade and dear friend. Later a man was shot dead here, in his own flat in Bedford Court, and among the belongings in that flat was all the evidence that he had killed these soldiers across India. While that London shooting stirred police interest, and Arjani assisted them, no one was very motivated to punish whoever had killed the soldiers' killer."

"And when was this, the Covent Garden shooting?" Holmes asked.

"Early 1860s," Watson said.

---

5. See Tennyson's "The Charge of the Light Brigade" (1854); Christina Rossetti's Skene lament; R. Kipling's work came later, but "The Young British Soldier" fits the mood.

By now, Holmes had lit his pipe. "Subsequent to the professor's arrival in London?"

"Oh yes," replied Watson, "a bit after that. And I didn't begin at Barts until '74."

UNKNOWN TO THE TWO he'd left at the Jugged Hare, Arjani did not return in the Hansom cab to his flat, but to No. 10 South Street, Mayfair, Florence Nightingale's home.

"A useful evening, Jehan?"

He recounted the facts to her. "Even if Holmes discovers finger-mark evidence of the thief's identity, he's faced with the dilemma that Scotland Yard will not concur."

"And did you keep your promise to me over John Watson's wounds? You didn't badger him about this artery business?"

Arjani conceded that he had not. "But I am concerned that he will move ahead with his intention to publish his memoirs — his 'reminiscences,' as he prefers to call them. After all, I set him on the road to combat medicine, and I don't wish him to be ridiculed by some hare-brained literary critic for his imprecision on anatomical detail. Is it possible that a single bullet fractured a bone in his shoulder and also injured that artery? Of course it is — though, as his anatomy instructor, I would prefer that he specify which bone. And you, above all people, Florence, will know that in the heat of battle, especially one you are losing, one's blood pressure and heart rate would be such that a wound to the subclavian artery would be undoubtedly fatal. He calls it a 'graze,' but it's impossible for the victim of the wound to know—"

"Yes, yes, Professor Arjani, we have, not to make a pun, dissected this argument already, so it's not—"

"I know, my dear, but you see how it will look for him, a trained surgeon, to misidentify such a wound and claim to have survived it, in a battle already proved to be an embarrassment to our Army. It will look silly in the press, and surely some half-baked newspaper hack will—"

"Enough, my darling surgical expert. Come to bed and teach me some anatomy."

Part III — Return to the Hare: Obstacles Removed

The luck to have Scotland Yard record Mandrake and his siblings' finger-marks prior to Christmas was not to be found. Indeed, it was mid-January before Holmes and Watson reunited with Arjani, once more at the Jugged Hare over pints of mulled cider.

"Have you been keeping well, Professor?" Watson inquired.

"Two nights past," Arjani replied, "Miss Nightingale and I attended a new Gilbert & Sullivan production at The Savoy — *Princess Ida*, not one of their best. Florence pronounced it *Princess Idle*. I believe it offended her sense of female achievement."

"She would know," Watson said. "One of the most renowned women in the Empire next to Her Majesty. You are a fortunate fellow, Professor."

"Very gracious of you, John, and you must join us soon for dinner. Florence has seen little of you since your return from Afghanistan and is very keen to renew the friendship. She recalls with great fondness our evening at the Opera Comique attending *HMS Pinafore.*"

"Most kind, most kind," said Watson, "and in the delightful company of Miss Colette Grafton-Higgs, as I recall. Rest assured, I will make the effort. But Holmes has some news for you."

"Indeed?" Arjani turned to Holmes. "Good or bad?"

"A bit of both," Holmes replied, "but mostly the former." He lit his pipe from the same match that Watson had just lit his. "There is a salient fact which I did not divulge to you at our last meeting, anticipating the findings of the three siblings' finger-marks, which were yet to be obtained directly by Scotland Yard or, if necessary, myself."

Arjani wanted to be patient. "And that was..."

"That the finger-mark data," Holmes said, "obtained by myself from the walnut chest and the two remaining jewelry pieces, and its subsequent analysis showed that, aside from Hollings, three individuals had handled the chest since its last polish by the maid.

"You see, I identified nineteen separate fingers and five thumbs. That's too many different marks for only two people, having sixteen fingers and four thumbs. Yet it's too few for four people, with thirty-two fingers and eight thumbs. "

Watson was beaming. "What did I tell you, Professor? A work of solitary precision!"

A part of Arjani's mind was astonished. The rest was hungry for more. "Hollings?"

"Yes," Holmes said, "he was eliminated by his foolproof alibi of rugby football. Hence, his marks on the box, six fingers and two thumbs, were also eliminated."

"Leaving three thumbs," Watson said gleefully, "and thirteen fingers."

"And the two additional jewelry pieces?" Arjani asked.

Holmes' self-satisfied smile was barely tolerable. "Those marks matched with the three plus thirteen from the chest, except for the loss of one finger and the addition of one thumb."

"And these were from the siblings?" Arjani wanted to know.

To Arjani's confusion, Watson was nearly beside himself with good humor, announcing, "We don't know."

"I will explain," Holmes said. "Please recall that my contact at Lloyd's reported to me that Mandrake had lodged an insurance claim with them for the missing items, alleging theft, but later discovered that a police report was required to accompany the claim."

"I do recall that," Arjani said, his patience intact, but strained.

"And that he then immediately canceled my investigation." Holmes's fingers formed a tent above his pint of cider. "Lloyd's contracts specify they will not reimburse for a theft if the thief is shown to be a family member and, thereby, a possible beneficiary of the claim. Now, suppose Mandrake got this fact from Lloyd's without revealing his suspicion of Rowena's probable guilt? He then invites Scotland Yard 'round to document the loss, and then cancels my involvement, so that my findings do not implicate Rowena and, thereby, nullify the claim at Lloyd's.

"Any details of this that I had not already deduced were explained to me by the Lloyd's agent at his desk in the Royal Exchange. Obviously, should Mandrake have realized he was, in the first instance, correct — that the thief was Rowena — and if I produced that evidence, there would be no insurance settlement, making his a total loss should she have already disposed of the jewelry. Hence, he decided to conspire with her to protect their coverage under Lloyd's by reporting to the police that the jewels had been stolen by someone outside the home. Based on that, and the police report, Lloyd's paid on the claim.

"When I subsequently explained to the agent my findings against an outside theft, he concurred, whereupon he retained me to prove the conclusion of a domestic crime."

"And that's the work — the data," said Arjani, "that you've been pursuing with the finger-marks on the chest and separate jewelry for many weeks?"

"Precisely," Watson said, "with Scotland Yard's knowledge but not collaboration."

"Once I had the data," Holmes said, "I presented it to Lloyd's. That was before Christmas."

Now Arjani was smiling, too. He understood. "But you did not yet have finger-marks taken directly from the siblings?"

"Correct," Holmes said. "However, with the findings I did have, Lloyd's called in the siblings after New Year to discuss 'progress on the case,' so to speak. It was explained to them how the detection science worked, and the purported reliability of fingertip patterns to identify individuals involved in a crime. As reality dawned, Rowena and Mandrake turned on each other, and the facts of their conspiracy were soon plain for all to see.

Mandrake returned most of his share of the insurance money and got a lighter prison sentence. Rowena had spent her share of the claim, as well as the proceeds from selling some of the jewelry, and so went away for a longer spell. The third sibling was not involved, a victim of the others' mendacity. She retained that part of the collection Rowena had not disposed of, which was determined to be at least a third of the lot."

"And the two remaining jewelry pieces?" Arjani asked.

"To the third sibling, as well," said Holmes, rattling his fingernails against the handle of his mug. "So, Mr. Arjani, I hope you derive some satisfaction from your contribution to the science of criminal detection."

The three were finishing their second pints of wassail by then, and Watson left to visit the WC.

Arjani remarked, "In the greater scheme, this seems a small matter, the rich stealing from the rich."

"But, sir," Holmes said, "the advancements that finger-marks have made will play a great part in the methodology and science of fighting crime."

Arjani provided a measured smile. "You have a most rewarding and entertaining tale here, Mr. Holmes. I am gratified to be part of finding justice for the unnamed sister and Lloyd's of London."

"And Lloyd's is expressing their gratitude, sir," Holmes said, "by buying your drinks tonight."[6]

---

6. No record shows the relation in value between Holmes's fee from Lloyd's on the Mayfair theft and the bar bill at the Jugged Hare.

Arjani nodded. "Most grateful, Mr. Holmes, but I have a question still."

Holmes glanced toward the WC, and then grinned, but only slightly. "I'm at your service, sir."

"I understand — that is, I understood — from John Watson that you have, on occasion, disappeared. Sometimes from the flat. Sometimes from the street. That he has no clear understanding how you do this, how it happens, and that you avoid speaking about it to him should a question arise."

For a moment, Holmes squeezed his lower lip under his front teeth. "And your question, Mr. Arjani?"

"I'd rather not be obtuse, Mr. Holmes. How do you do it, or how do you convince Watson that you do it?"

At this moment, Holmes looked up to see his companion returning to their table. He held back any answer until Watson was seated. After a brief moment, Holmes looked at Watson, Watson looked at him, and Arjani watched Holmes pass an open hand across Watson's eyes. Watson's face lost all expression. His lips closed a fraction and touched. His eyes blinked once and then went slack. Holmes laid his right hand gently on Watson's left wrist and then rose from the table and walked toward the bar.

Once he was out of Watson's field of vision, Watson turned to Arjani and said, "Has Holmes left us?" Then he turned again, looking toward Holmes and the barman, saying, "Has he left the pub and gone home?" obviously not perceiving the man with whom he shared a Baker Street flat.

Arjani had no intention of evading the question, of abandoning Watson to this strange notion, but was lost for an immediate answer. Just then, Holmes returned and, from behind, laid his right hand on Watson's right shoulder. Watson's eyes flicked, his lips twitched, and his head raised and swiveled.

"Ah, Holmes, there you are. I thought you'd disappeared again."

Looking up into Holmes's somber face, Arjani said, "As did I, Mr. Holmes. Obviously, we have much to discuss."

—THE END—

About the Author

Lance Mason's writing reflects both his origins in rural California and his extensive travel abroad. He has explored, lived, and worked overseas for decades, traveling the world by foot, bicycle, and motorcycle, train, plane, and dugout canoe, including 15 years in New Zealand, experiences that have both enhanced and interfered with Mason's writing life. His work has appeared in 50+ journals, collections, anthologies, etc., was included in Fish Publishing's 2025 Memoir Prize (Ireland), received a Silver and two Golds in the 2024 and '25 Solas Awards, and his fiction recently appeared in *ShortStoryStack* (Palisatrium), Eerie River's BLADES, and Cowboy Jamboree's PRINE PRIMED, among others.

Learn more at www.facebook.com/AuthorLMason/ and at x.com/lance_mason_com.

The Four-Minute Man

By Tom Barlow

LEFTY SHAW COULDN'T HAVE been more pleased with the audience, gathered to see the debut of *Tarzan of the Apes* and *The Ghost of Slumber Mountain*. Silent movies were the primary entertainment in 1918 for this little cow town on the Iowa prairie. The manager knew of Four-Minute Men, hawking the war bonds crucial to funding the Great War in Europe, but he resented having to yield the house to someone from out of town for the pitch, even when Lefty produced a letter identifying himself as an official speaker for the federal Committee on Public Information. Lefty prevailed when he subtly suggested the manager's loyalty might come into question if he didn't capitulate.

"OK, folks," Lefty said, falling into his four-minute patter. "Fritz isn't fooling around, is he? This so-called Spanish flu, do you really believe it is a coincidence that it has appeared just at the moment our troops are getting the upper hand in the war?"

The crowd muttered; the flu hadn't reached Paulding yet, but most of the country's rural areas now figured it was just a matter of time, after the way it had destroyed so many big cities like Philadelphia and ravaged the Army training bases set up to handle the boys who had been drafted to fight the war.

"Right now, there are boys waiting for hospital beds in France." Lefty scanned the crowd, making eye contact. "While you sit here, well off enough to go to the motion pictures," he added a nuance of scorn to his voice, "they're dying in mud ditches. Mud ditches, with barely enough ammunition and food and few gas masks. How do you expect Mr. Wilson to win this war for us with empty pockets? I'm telling you, folks, I can't believe any real American would rather spend money on an hour or two in the movie house than buy war bonds. And here's the great thing about the bonds; you'll get your money back, and more, after we drive Fritz back where he belongs." He could see that his words were working on the men in the audience. "You, sir," he said, pointing to a middle-aged farmer in the center of the audience, "you have any boys in the Army?"

Everyone turned to look at him. "My eldest, Tyrone, is up at Camp Dodge, but he's been sick as a dog. What's the Army doing to keep our boys safe?"

"Blame the Huns, sir. It must be Hun-lovers calling this the Spanish flu, when we know for a fact that it is the Germans who are responsible. What can you do to pay them back? Buy war bonds. Save your money after we win the war, but now, if you have an extra five bucks, President Wilson needs it. You can see me in the lobby between the shows, and I expect every one of you to do the right thing by your country. Thanks for your time."

He gave the audience a thumbs-up as he walked the aisle to the lobby, the brace on his knee reminding him to limp badly; healthy men his age were expected to join up without waiting to be drafted.

The manager had rustled up a table and chair for Lefty. He laid out his supplies and thumbtacked a poster for the bonds on the wall behind him. He'd seen the films a couple of times, so instead of joining the audience he took the air outside. The small farming community was shut down except for the theater, and the stable next door, where the horses were nervous. The usual Plains August thunderstorm was building in the west.

The door opened and the manager exited, looking around until he spotted Lefty. The man wore a tux and his florid complexion suggested he could stroke out in the heat at any moment. He lit a cigarette and said, "Where you from? You don't sound like an Iowa man."

"Minnesota. That's the Viking accent coming through. You live in town?"

"I'm the mayor. Willie Bradstreet. You know, my brother's bank across the street sells war bonds. I don't know as I like the idea of an outsider poaching his business."

Lefty had sweated through a number of such confrontations before he gained the confidence to deal with them. "The CPI sends men like me around because it's hard for a man to ask a friend for money. I can come in here and I don't have any relationships to risk. You'd be surprised how much money I can liberate from a crowd like this."

The mayor pursed his lips. "I suppose you have some identification? I mean, beyond that letter you showed me."

"Of course." He pulled out the endorsement from the CPL that identified Cornelius Shaw as a Field Representative for Iowa, Nebraska, Minnesota, and the Dakotas. He'd paid the forger extra for the foil embossment on it along with three other endorsements with different identities, and they were worth every cent.

The mayor held the document up, tilted it to read by the moonlight and ran his finger across the embossed foil before handing it back. "Well, I guess that's OK. But there's no use staying around for another day. About everybody in a ten-mile radius is here tonight, so any audience tomorrow will be the same people. Some of them come every night, see the same moving pictures over and over. It's either here or go to church. You have a good night." He reentered the theater.

Lefty was pleasantly surprised at the line in the lobby after the first film ended and the organist launched into "Over There." Not any one person shocked him with a twenty, but the basic five-dollar purchases added up to a nice kitty. He handed each customer a miniature American flag along with their stamp. He managed to empty a book of the "war bond stamps" that a down-on-his-luck printer in St. Louis had printed for him. Those stamps and flags had cost him, but brother, he'd made a lot of dough with them. A grifter was only as good as his props.

THE NEW AMERICA HOTEL was the only place to stay in town. He'd taken a room earlier that day on arrival and returned famished. While they had held a supper for him, he found that they still abided by the Meatless Tuesdays that Wilson had advocated after the droughts of '16 and '17. The bean soup, made without ham bones, tasted like a bowl of plaster. The dumplings were too dense for his teeth, one of which was about ready to pull.

The only redeeming feature was the cute woman who brought his meal to the table. She was on the thin side, but with square shoulders and prominent breasts. He guessed her age at maybe twenty, ten years his junior. She wore a touch of makeup to accentuate her best features, cornflower eyes, dimples, and full lips. He normally kept his distance from local women, fearing they would queer his scam, but he hadn't been back home to St. Paul to visit his wife in three months and his libido was yelling bloody murder.

He was the only customer in the dining room this late, and he was surprised and pleased when she said, "Mind if I join you? My feet are killing me. The cook's gone, so nobody's going to know."

He gestured to the chair opposite, and she took a seat. "I'm Rachael, by the way."

He introduced himself, giving her the sheepish smile that suggested he was on the shy side. It worked like magic on vulnerable women. The way she leaned forward, one elbow on the table, suggested she was vulnerable.

"Tell me about Paulding," he said as he scraped the bottom of the bowl. Just because it was tasteless didn't mean he was willing to go hungry.

"Not much to tell," she replied, fishing a cigarette from her apron. He took the lighter from his vest pocket and lit it for her. "If you care about corn and pork, you'll never run out of conversation. If you want to talk culture, you're out of luck."

"You grow up here?"

She was a little flushed. "Yeah, but I'll be darned if I'll die here."

"If you could live anywhere?" he said.

"Maybe Chicago, or New York, or Paris. But this darn war, it's messed up everything."

"You had plans?"

"My cousin was going to get a job in Chicago and rent me a room there once he found a place to live. Instead, he got drafted. He was killed in France the day after he arrived."

There was a bitterness in her voice that suggested she was fed up with her life as it currently stood. Although he knew the danger, he could not help but take advantage of her discontent. There was nothing about his appearance that would put her off, and he had a practiced seduction patter that seldom failed.

———

HE WOKE IN HIS room later than night, sleepily aware that Rachael was no longer stretched out beside him, so he presumed she had gone home. She had been clear that she wasn't the kind of woman to sleep around, and she had followed him to his room only because he was a stranger and would be gone in the morning.

However, he caught a whiff of cigarette smoke and turned to find her seated in the straight chair on the window side of the bed. She had dressed, and moonlight shone on her lap. There rested the paperwork for the four identities he kept in his luggage in case he needed a new name in a hurry.

"Cornelius Shaw," she said. "Theodore Baker. Andrew Simmons. Abraham Gamble. That last one is ironic, don't you think? You take a gamble every time you steal a town's worth of patriotism. And your leg? It gave you no problem last night, with the brace off."

"It's not what you think," he said, sitting up in bed and turning on the lamp.

"It's exactly what I think," she said. "My cousin died in France and who knows — maybe if the Army had the money you stole, he'd still be alive. My dad is the Chief of Police. My uncle is the Mayor of Paulding. I don't envy you if I show them this stuff."

Lefty had spent three years in the Ohio Pen for running the money-box scheme in Dayton, and he'd vowed the day he got out that he'd do anything to keep from returning. "I took in sixty bucks last night," he said. "Take it. All I'm asking for is a head start to get out of town."

"You're not going anywhere without me," she said, lifting the papers and pointing them at him. "This here is my lucky break. You see, the richest guy in the county is Byron Lewinsky. He owns the pork processing plant. His son Walter was the football hero, here and up at Iowa State. Everybody in town, including my family, his family, loves Walter and expects me to marry him, and Walter is more than willing. His old man has made noises about maybe moving his business to Des Moines, but the townspeople figure if I pump out a dozen or so little Walters the family will be so invested in the county they would never consider leaving, taking with them all those jobs."

"So what's the problem?"

"The problem is Walter's a pig himself." She flicked her cigarette butt out the window. "The only reason he needs a wife is to polish his trophies and procreate. If I stay here, when he returns from France, they'll drag me to the altar whether I like it or not, and I'll be darned if I'm going to live that kind of life. I have ambitions of my own. That's why I'm leaving with you, like it or not."

"You don't know what you're asking. I'm on the move every day or two. I don't have a permanent home."

"I'm not proposing we marry. You're going to drive me to the train station in Chicago. With your sixty dollars and what I have stashed away, I can go anywhere in the country from there. Then you can return to robbing people since that seems to be what you do best. You're sure not good enough in bed to find yourself a rich widow. Four-minute man, indeed."

He ignored the jibe. "Why not catch a train in Rochester? It's only twenty miles away."

"Because my cousin Elbert is the station master there and he's not going to let me get away. You don't know my dad; he thinks he owns his children, and he'll go to any length to keep me under his thumb. The rest of the family is happy to cooperate."

"So, he'll come after you when he sees you're gone?" He stood and began to dress.

"For sure. I forgot to mention, you're going to set me up with a new identity before you go. I like the name Lillian. Or maybe Clara. Thompson."

Lefty picked up his pocket watch and checked the time. Two a.m. He had no intention of driving this woman to Chicago, not that his old Model T would even make it that far, certainly not on what served for roads in Iowa. He'd been fixing flats every hour or two. He wasn't about to become the focus of some dragnet looking for this woman, either, if she was under such scrutiny. He figured he would drive her east until she needed to take a comfort break in a cornfield, then drive off and leave her there for them to find. Since she was a woman, surely she would need to stop within the hour, given the jostling the road would provide.

"If we're going, you better get your stuff," he said. "You live close?"

"Upstairs. They converted the third floor into apartments last year. You come on up, too; you're not getting out of my sight." She rolled the documents and stuffed them in her purse.

With his wife as an example, Lefty expected Rachel to take a couple of hours packing. To his surprise, she was already mostly packed. "I been looking for a way out for a month now," she said. "They caught me once, waiting for the bus when I thought they were all at a funeral for the church pastor. I never been talked to that way before." He was disappointed when she took the time to use the restroom before they left.

They passed through the kitchen to avoid the front desk. The door on the loading dock exited into the alley. The town was as still as the cornfields surrounding it.

They circled the building to the parking lot on the side where his car sat next to a hitching post. He tossed the luggage into the back of his sedan and helped her into the passenger seat. He engaged the emergency brake, returned to the front of the car, pulled the choke, and gave the crank a quarter turn, praying it would start. Thankfully, it caught, hiccupping a few times while it warmed up enough to burn the kerosene efficiently.

"Hurry up," Rachel said. "They can hear your jalopy all across town."

He hopped in and decided to delay turning on the headlamps, as the half moon was bright enough to navigate by. As they passed the police department, though, the front door opened, and a figure peered out from the lit interior.

As soon as they were clear of town, headed east, he turned on his headlamps. Over the clattering of the engine, he could hear Rachel laughing.

"What's so funny?"

"I'm just imagining the look on their faces when they finally figure out I'm gone."

"They'll be furious, won't they?"

She playfully slapped at his shoulder. "Not at me. I left a note in lipstick on the bathroom mirror saying you'd kidnapped me. For insurance, in case they caught up with us."

"What?" The car slipped into a rut, and he struggled to keep the steering wheel secure in his grip. "Why in hell's name did you do that? They'll have every cop in Iowa out after us now."

"Don't be silly. They won't find the note until tomorrow; I'm not scheduled to work today, so no one is going to miss me. By then, we should be in Chicago. Isn't that right?"

"Right. Then you disappear and they'll never stop looking for me. They'll probably figure I killed you and buried you in some cornfield."

"You get me to Chicago, I'll telegraph my uncle and let him know I'm OK. You ditch me before then and I'll tell the world about your scam. There won't be no place for you to hide."

"You messaging your dad won't stop him from looking for me, if only to find out where I took you."

Lefty had never been behind the eight ball like this before. If they caught him, his con would surely be exposed, and that meant another, even longer stretch in prison. And even if he beat that rap, chances are his wife would find out he'd been cheating on her. On their wedding day, her father had threatened to cut him if he ever did her wrong.

In the pen, his cellmate was a fellow who figured he knew it all, and one thing he knew kept running through Lefty's head; "Most losers get caught because they don't have the guts to do the hard thing that would keep them free." His cellmate hadn't had the guts to throw his wife out their tenth-floor window and claim it suicide. If he had, she would never have squealed on him.

Lefty couldn't let go the thought that his life was about to hit the skids, and how unfair it was that this woman who he barely even knew was going to make it happen. He stewed over that for a few more miles until finally, on a stretch of road bordered by six-foot stands of corn, he came to a hard decision. He brought the car to a stop.

"What? You got to tinkle?" Rachael said.

He opened his pocket watch and held it up to the moon. Three a.m. He took a deep breath as he put it away and let his left hand drop down to where he kept a wrench between the seat and the car door. "You've put me in an impossible situation, don't you get that? You leave me no choice." He threw his right arm across her chest to hold her arms down as he swung the wrench with his left. It connected squarely with her temple and her skull caved in. She began to shake as blood exploded from the wound, but only for a minute before the life faded from her eyes.

Lefty stepped out of the car and stood there for a couple of minutes, trying to get used to the idea of himself as a killer, before settling down enough to review the harebrained scheme he had come up with. A longshot, but he could think of nothing better. He finally reentered the car, turned it around, and headed back toward Paulding.

HE DROVE DUE WEST until he could see the town water tower in the distance, then turned south onto an intersecting road and parked at the end of the cornfield. The moon hung low in the sky as he hefted Rachel onto his shoulder and entered the field, walking down a row parallel to the road into town. He couldn't risk being seen, even though the countryside was still dead quiet. Adrenalin kept him moving through the hot and sticky night. He paused several times to rest and catch his breath before reaching town and the alley that ran behind the hotel.

Thankfully, the loading dock door was still unlocked, so he could carry Rachel's body up to the second floor landing unobserved. He left her there then climbed up to her room to erase the note on the bathroom mirror.

There was no note.

Furious, he returned to her body and carefully posed it as though she had fallen down the stairs and hit her head. He had to squeeze the head wound to cause some blood to flow out onto the edge of the bottom stair. He could do nothing about the lack of a suitcase. He only hoped no one would notice.

He exited the building via the kitchen again and set off toward his car, wishing he had knocked down a couple of stalks to mark the row he'd followed in. As he headed out of town, the moon was down but the sky was not quite as dark as it had been. He had to hurry.

But hurrying had its price. The corn leaves were just thin and stiff enough that, when he caught one in the face, it left a little nick. Soon he bled from a dozen cuts. In the field, the heat was climbing, even in the cool of pre-dawn; sweat poured off his forehead. The soil provided uneven footing, too, so he repeatedly stumbled, and his straw hat was grabbed by a corn stalk every few minutes.

He seemed to have walked a greater distance than he remembered, which he wrote off to his state of mind, until he emerged from the cornfield onto a road to find no car. He looked up — the sky was growing light to his left, telling him the row he had followed had bent gradually south with the contour of the land, while his car was still due east of town. Cursing, he headed back toward Paulding, where he could hopefully catch the right corn row.

By the time he emerged behind the hotel, the sun was just below the horizon, and he could see clearly enough to locate his footprints and determine the correct corn row. He set off east toward his car. The heat was his enemy now. He took off his jacket, his tie, his collar, but still sweated like a draft horse as he passed down the row. After what seemed like an eternity, he finally spotted the front door of his car ahead.

A cop was leaning up against it, looking the other way.

Lefty quickly cut south several rows until he was out of the cop's sight. Was the man looking for Lefty, or did he just stumble upon the abandoned car? Lefty wouldn't be able to convince the cop his foray into the field was innocent, not with all that blood on the seat. He had to believe they'd see through his subterfuge now and link him to Rachel's death. The only alternative he could think of was to make his way to Rochester and catch the train. They'd be watching the ticket window, but maybe he could sneak into a boxcar. He could walk the twenty miles to the station in no more than eight hours. He was reasonably fit, although he had a limp from his habit of wearing the brace.

He cut north through the corn until he could cross the main east-west road out of Paulding. He entered another cornfield and kept heading north toward Rochester.

AN HOUR LATER, THIRST had become his biggest concern. The only liquid he had was a pint of whiskey in his jacket pocket, and one swallow of that convinced him booze was no remedy. He was allergic to something in the field, too. He was coughing up a storm.

He waited at the end of each field to make sure the coast was clear before crossing the road. He feared the authorities were searching for him already, as he could see dust clouds rising off the dirt roads around him.

By noon, Lefty had made maybe ten miles, but he was exhausted. While the air temperature was appreciably higher, he could not control his shivering. Still, he shuffled on and on. At some point, he lost his hat, at some point he took off his vest, then his shirt, though when he didn't quite remember.

At long last, he found some water pooled in a ditch alongside the road. Although it was covered in slime, he skimmed off the crust and leaned down until he could scoop up some of the water. It was warm and tasted like rotten fish, but it was wet. He made himself take a deep drink.

He was on his knees, vomiting uncontrollably, when the Paulding Chief of Police rolled up in his paddy wagon.

"I'VE GOT THAT FLU," he said to the Chief after he finished emptying his stomach. "I need a doctor and fast. I heard of men dying in eight hours."

"That's too bad. Get in." The back door of the paddy wagon was already open.

"Why? I haven't done anything."

"You know what you did." The Chief reached out with his nightstick and rapped him hard on the shoulder. "Git."

Lefty barely remembered the ride back to Paulding; he hallucinated Rachel seated across from him, not talking, just glaring. And the bouncing of the paddy wagon caused his muscles to hurt like he'd never hurt before. He was relieved when they pulled up in front of the police station.

The Chief opened the door. "Get out."

Lefty fell flat on the ground when he attempted to step down. The Chief stood six feet away with pistol drawn. "Get off your keister or I'll plug you where you lie."

Lefty could read the fury in his eyes and rose to his feet.

The Chief said, "Walk over to the flagpole."

The twenty-foot steel flagpole stood in the small yard in front of the station. Puzzled, Lefty followed his direction.

Once there, the Chief said, "Put your back up against the pole and your hands behind you."

The Chief circled behind and slapped a pair of handcuffs on him, connected by a heavy chain, trapping him to the pole. "You just stay out here. You're not getting anywhere near people so you can give them your flu."

"You can't leave me out here in the sun," Lefty said. "I'll roast."

"You shouldn't have killed my daughter. Nobody in town is going to have any mercy for you now."

"I never. Last time I saw her she was fine."

"Don't bother. The night dispatcher saw her leave in the car with you. Then she's back here and dead? There's all that blood in your car, and her luggage is in the back. Don't take me for a fool."

The Chief went inside, but a moment later his clerk came out with a folding chair and took up a position a good twenty feet away. She wore a bandana over her nose and mouth.

"You here to make sure I don't escape?" Lefty said.

"I'm here to keep people from punching you in the mouth," she said. "We don't want them getting the flu by doing so."

All through the morning, he felt worse and worse: body aches, fever, the chills, and coughing jags that went on for five minutes at a time. He begged for water, but the clerk just shook her head. She did chase off a child who was chucking rocks at him, but not before he landed one on the back of Lefty's head. A soldier in his khaki uniform approached to within six feet and managed to hit him with a gob of spit before the clerk ran him off, too.

By noon, a steady stream of people had passed on the opposite sidewalk, all glowering at him. Some shouted to the clerk, asking why they didn't just hang him. One offered to donate the rope and the use of his elm tree.

By the time the bell in the Methodist Church rang three o'clock, Lefty could no longer sit. As he sprawled at the foot of the flagpole, his breathing ragged, the Chief came around the side of the building carrying an armful of firewood, which he dropped a few feet from Lefty.

"What's that for?" Lefty said.

The Chief dusted the bark off his sleeves. "After you go, we're going to burn your body. Nobody's willing to handle it until it's been sterilized. That's what we had to do with our hogs back in the hoof-and-mouth outbreak of '14, and that seemed to work OK."

"You're going to burn me after I die?" Lefty said, appalled.

"Yeah, that's the plan," the Chief said. "In fact, we've got it scheduled for six p.m. A lot of people want to watch, but there's a barnstorming baseball team here to play our town team at seven."

"But what if I'm not dead yet?"

"Then you'll get an early taste of hell."

At five o'clock, as he breathed his last, Lefty had a final thought; for the first time in his grifting career, he'd let an audience slip through his fingers.

—THE END—

About the Author

Tom Barlow is an American author of crime and mystery stories. His works have appeared in many journals including *Needle, Switchblade, Tough, Mystery Weekly*, and *Mystery Tribune*. His story "Smothered and Covered" appeared in *Best American*

Mystery Stories. He is the author of mystery novels *Blood of the Poppy* and *Everything is Inevitable* and the short story collection *Odds of Survival.* Learn more at www.tombarlowauthor.com.

Boy in a Box

By Dennis McFadden

"Ten Year Old Boy Wanders From Home"
— *Brookville American,* May 15, 1918

He emerged from the dappled shade of the hillside woods onto Hunts Alley, the packed dirt lane that ran along the north side of Redbank Creek. It had been a pretty walk down through the woods, the blue May sky peeking through new leaves, the air fresh and warm and clean, making Andy think of the garden. The last hymn he'd heard at Sunday School that morning kept playing in his mind: *I come to the Garden alone / While the dew is still on the roses...*

Then he saw the congregation of boys at the swimming hole.

They saw him, too. They watched him start down through the clearing toward where they were playing and swimming in the creek: Andy Clinger. He was small for ten, frail and light as a dandelion puff, yellow hair, big ears. He moved like a mouse in the shadow of a cat. The boys were about Andy's age, a few were older. They huddled, talking in hoarse whispers. Coming closer, Andy saw them clustered, glancing his way, grinning and talking. Plotting. He was wary. He'd been picked on enough to know they were not plotting to give him cookies and cream.

He changed his mind, changed his course, turned back up toward the lane.

The boys called after him: Andy! Hey Andy! Where you going? Yoo hoo, Andy! Don't you want to go swimming? Andy! C'mon in, the water's fine!

Andy was wise to them. He stepped on one of the big rocks scattered along the bank above the creek, turned his back to the boys, and dropped his pants. *Kiss my bum*, he hollered over his shoulder.

Pulling up his pants, he headed toward the lane again. A friend of his father's, Mr. Schwab, was just passing by in his gig, and Andy could see the look of dark disapproval on his face, having witnessed him baring his bum. His pony, on the other hand, tossed his head and nickered as though sniggering at the boy's antics.

According to the police report, this was the last time anyone, except for his killer, saw Andy Clinger alive.

WHAT THE POLICE REPORT didn't show: As soon as Mr. Schwab was out of sight, two of the boys took off after Andy, catching him quickly. Andy fought back, kicking and hitting, but he was no match for two bigger boys.

"Let me go, let me go! You're gonna be in big trouble!"

They carried him back down through the clearing to the swimming hole, one boy clasping his ankles, the other his wrists. On the bank, they swung him to and fro, a chorus of boys counting *One! Two! Three!* then heaved him into the deep pool in the middle of the stream, the water cold and high from the spring run-off. Surfacing, Andy splashed his way toward the bank where the boys were hooting and hollering. His face was red and twisted, ready to cry, but he held it in the best he could.

"You got my clothes all wet!" He splashed at the water in frustration and fury.

"We got his clothes all wet!" yelled one of the boys. "Heavens to Betsy!"

"He can't hardly wear wet clothes," hollered another. "He might catch his death!"

They seized him again, yanking off his sweater, then his pants and underpants, leaving him naked. "Gimme those!" shouted Andy. "Gimme those back!"

His clothes were tossed from boy to boy, waved about like banners.

"I'm gonna tell!" Andy stomped and splashed in frustration.

The cacophony of derision rose higher, drowning out his protests. Andy reached down to the stream bed, found rocks, and began flinging them blindly at the boys, one or two of which found soft flesh and hard bones. The boys retreated, still laughing, still hooting, still waving Andy's sweater and pants and underpants above their heads. They ran back across the clearing, scattering down the alley and into the woods, leaving Andy naked and shivering in the cold stream waters. He made his way to the bank of the creek.

Alone, he was free to cry to his heart's content.

—————

THE WORST OF HIS weeping was over when he heard a soft footfall behind him. Ben had come back. Turning, Andy saw him, head lowered sheepishly. Like most of the boys, he was bigger than Andy, a head taller, black curly hair and dark eyes that glimmered. His face had a kittenish quality, soft and flinching at every loud noise or perceivable threat. "Andy?"

Andy snuffled. "What do *you* want?" He quickly wiped his eyes.

Ben politely looked away, downstream. "You okay?"

"Oh, I'm just dandy. Except for the fact I'm sitting here buck naked."

"That was mean. I didn't think they'd..."

"I didn't see you try to stop them."

Ben had been with the pack of boys. True, he'd been on the periphery, not among the hollerers and hooters, certainly not a ringleader, but Andy felt betrayed nonetheless. He was the closest Andy had to a best friend. *Mutt and Jeff* the other kids called them. They'd been to each other's houses. They'd played cowboys and Indians; together they'd mowed down Huns from Andy's front porch. He'd given Ben a brand-new set of marbles in a leather pouch for his birthday, and this was how he had repaid him.

"What was I supposed to do? They'd have just ganged up on me."

"You're bigger than them!"

"They had me outnumbered, like a hundred to one."

"You could have *tried*."

"I didn't want to get in your way." Ben skipped a rock into the stream, the splashes quickly washed away by the water rippling over the rocks. He nodded his head slowly, sagely. "You looked like you had it pretty well under control."

"Hahaha. You're funnier than a barrel of monkeys."

"I figured if you'd thrown about two more stones, they'd have surrendered."

"Hahaha."

"At least you chased them off. Right?"

"Yeah. Them and all my clothes."

"Want me to go up to your place and get you some clothes?"

Andy said no. He didn't want his folks to know. "How about getting me something of yours? Something old you don't wear anymore?"

"What am I going to tell *my* folks?"

"I really don't care! I need something to wear!"

"Hey! You're a poet and you just don't know it!"

"Don't say it!" Andy put his hands over his ears.

"Except for your feet — they're long fellows!"

Ben's chuckle died on the vine when Andy only glared. "You gonna help me or not?"

They decided: Ben would go home and smuggle out some clothes. As fast as he could. Someone might come by any moment. Andy would stay hidden. But, just in case, he asked Ben if he could borrow his underpants.

"My underpants? I guess so. You sure?"

"Sure I'm sure. Why wouldn't I be sure? At least I'd have something on."

"Well, I'm not sure how clean they are."

Andy grimaced as though taking his cod liver oil. "I'll wash 'em out good in the creek."

ANDY WAITED, COLD AND shivering on the bank, glancing up and down the creek, behind him to the clearing and the woods on the hillside, and across the creek to the woods on the far bank. A woodpecker commenced hammering somewhere in the tall trees. Andy was fretful. Someone might come along. Thank God for the underpants, at least. At Sunday School that morning he'd also thanked God, but he couldn't remember what for. Underpants was as good a thing as any. He had to chuckle to himself at the very thought of thanking God for underpants, and, as he did, the hymn popped up again: *I come to the Garden alone / While the dew is still on the roses...* He looked around again. It felt as though the world was holding its breath. *And He walks with me and He talks with me / And He tells me I am his own...* A squirrel emerged from the brambles on the far bank, sat up straight in the weeds and stared at him, fat cheeks chewing. Overhead, the sky was deep blue, a puffy white cloud here and there, birds soaring and dipping and soaring.

He watched the water roll over the rocks. Waiting. *Tarrying.*

And the joy we share as we tarry there / None other has ever known...

He heard footsteps behind him.

***Ben lived with his father in a big house on Walnut Street, not far from Andy's place on Jenks. His mother had died when he was three, an accidental drowning. He could barely remember her. His father would try to chat, as he often did, to pass a little time with his son, to make up for all the hours, day and night, he spent at the office. He would ask Ben what he was up to.

Ben lined up his lies.

But when he got to the door, his father was just stepping out. He was fresh-shaven and clean-smelling, dapper as usual in his well-pressed pinstriped suit and vest. Ben had gotten his black curly hair and hard cheekbones from his father, who seemed to be smiling a secret smile. "Ben. What's up, son? I was just leaving." He hesitated, as if deciding something.

Ben was not one to look a gift horse in the mouth. The last thing he would do is ask his father where he was going and risk a conversation. "See you later," he said.

His father started to stammer a response, changed his mind, smiled, and was off.

In his room Ben found an old pair of britches, threadbare, holes in the knees, and an even older yellow jersey, the smallest he could find, the oldest and most worn-out as well. He folded them into a small bundle and headed back down the stairs.

Headed straight back down toward the creek.

A handful of boys was back, skipping rocks and wrestling in the dirt. But not Andy. Andy was nowhere to be seen.

———

ANDY LOOKED INTO THE eyes of his killer with blank com-prehension — it was wrong, it was insane, it was impossible. His blood raced, temples pounding. Above, beyond the face of his killer, the blue sky turned splotchy and white, birds darting across it like someone flinging mud. His heart was thumping, rampaging, bludgeoning its way through his skinny body, ham-mering his brain, blinding him, soaring out of his body and up into the air with the splotches and mud.

He walks with me and He talks with me / And He tells me I am his own...

The words of the hymn were too fast, racing faster and faster, gushing, not the way they were supposed to be. *And the joy we share as we tarry there / None other has ever known!* faster and faster, whirling, blending into one hollow, echoing roar.

And the joy we share as we tarry there...

Now I lay me down to sleep...

———

BEN SEARCHED. UP AND down the creek in both directions, behind big rocks and fallen logs and in gullies where Andy, embarrassed wearing only oversized underpants, might have ducked to hide. Maybe he fell asleep; Ben knew him to be a sound sleeper. He looked in outhouses, sheds and other out-buildings, even in a doghouse or two. He searched for a long time. The last place he looked was in the overgrown tennis court on the wooded, downhill side of Franklin Street where he and Andy had hollowed out a clearing in the middle of the brambles and bushes and called it their clubhouse.

When he showed up at Andy's house toward the end of the afternoon, he was surprised to find the door locked. The door was never locked. He knocked, waited, knocked again. When Mrs. Clinger finally answered, she looked annoyed. And disheveled. Had she been napping?

"Why is the door locked?" Ben said.

"Ben, what do you want?" Her hair was limp and damp, a wayward curl twisting down her forehead. Oh boy. She was in one of her moods. Ben didn't risk eye contact.

"Andy. Is he here? I can't find him anywhere." He looked at his feet.

"That's because he went to Harmony Mills with his father."

"No, he didn't," said Ben, cringing a little. "He was at the swimming hole earlier."

"Oh? You're sure about that, are you?" She cocked her head and looked at him as though he were a puppy who'd just pooped on the floor.

"Yes. I saw him with my own two eyes." Ben thought he caught a whiff coming from inside, a whiff of something that smelled familiar.

"As far as I'm concerned, he's in Harmony Mills. With his father. Goodbye, Ben."

With that, she shut the door in Ben's face.

Odd. It had seemed as though Mrs. Clinger wasn't really interested in what Ben had to say — but what could be more important than Andy's whereabouts, even if she wasn't Andy's real mother (which just about everybody in town knew by now)? It wasn't until later, four or five days later, well after Mr. Clinger had returned home (without Andy) from his Association of Episcopal Deacons meeting in Harmony Mills, well after Andy had been officially reported missing, after the creek had been dragged and search parties had scoured the hills and woods for miles around, after all the boys who'd been at the creek had been questioned, after telephone messages had been sent to surrounding officials, it wasn't until after all that had occurred that Darryl Johns — one of the older boys who'd thrown Andy into the creek that Sunday afternoon — saw Ben down on Main Street and hollered, "Hey, Ben — I hear your old man's porking Andy's mother!" And the familiar smell he'd smelled at Andy's began to fall into place.

Ben's face flinched like a kitten's, and he pretended he hadn't heard Darryl. He went on about his business, into Sterck's to take the measure of the new comic books that had come in. He was pretty sure he knew what *porking* meant. He leafed through the new *Krazy Kat* blindly, Darryl's words tumbling in his head. Had Andy known about it, too?

He'd been acting oddly. The last time they met at their clubhouse in the overgrown tennis court a couple of weeks ago, Andy brought a new comic book, *Gasoline Alley*, but only leafed through it, not really taking it in. Ben wanted to play army. He'd spied a Kraut patrol just the other side of Coal Alley where much of the hillside was trees and undergrowth — plenty of ambush spots for sneaky Huns — but Andy wasn't interested in that, either.

Andy was lost in thought. Ben was restless. Andy sat, his arms hugging his knees, staring out through the gaps in the undergrowth at the high white dome atop the Courthouse. From the hillside where they sat, the dome that towered over Main Street was just about eye level. Beyond that, on the far hillside, the tarnished steeple of the Catholic church jutted toward heaven.

"I hate my mother." Andy, still staring down at the town, didn't turn around when he said this.

Ben was not particularly surprised. "Frances or your real mother?"

"What do you think, dummy?"

"Frances." The family had tried to keep it under wraps at first, ten years ago, but in a small town like Hartsgrove, word was bound to seep out. The Clingers, Frances and Harry, were not Andy's real parents. His real mother was his "Aunt" Vera, Mr. Clinger's baby sister. No one knew who his real father was, except maybe Vera. Or maybe not. She might well not know. Ben had heard Mr. Clinger, and others, describe her as *slow*. Slow? Maybe, Ben thought, but he liked her. Andy loved her. He'd rather live with Vera, his real mom, at her cottage just down from Clinger's house, instead of with his uncle and stepmother, masquerading as his parents. But Mr. Clinger wouldn't hear of it. Appearances matter. What's more, his baby sister hadn't the means to properly care for Andy. It would be like two children living on their own, he said.

"Why?" Ben said. "Why do you hate Frances?"

"Why do you think?"

"Because she hates you?"

Andy's narrow shoulders gave a giant shrug. "So what? Everybody hates me."

Andy had once asked Ben why everyone picked on him, while no one picked on Ben. *Easy*, Ben had told him. *You're little and mouthy, and I'm big and not.* There was something in Andy that wouldn't let him learn that simple lesson.

"Oh, I wouldn't say everybody hates you." Ben tried to look at Andy, but he didn't turn around, still staring across town to the far hillside. He noticed Andy's ears, from behind, looked even bigger. They seemed to let the light shine through.

"Oh, yeah? Who doesn't hate me?"

"Let's see," said Ben. "Let me think. There's, uh... no, he hates your guts. But there's always, golly, no, he really can't stand you either. How about... no, he can't stand the sight of you either. Let me think... there's gotta be somebody..."

Andy turned, brow knotted like a fist. "You are so funny. Ha. Ha. Ha."

"Okay, okay. *I* don't hate you," Ben said. Andy rolled his eyes. "You get on my nerves a lot, but I don't *hate* you."

ON THE EVENING OF the day Andy went missing, well before his Main Street encounter with Darryl Hidinger, before the authorities had even been notified, Ben had gone to see Andy's mother — his real mother, "Aunt" Vera. If anyone knew where Andy was, she well might.

"No," she said when Ben asked. "Something's happened to him."

Ben thought it was a question. "I don't know for sure, but—"

"No, no," she said. "Something's *happened* to him."

"How do you know?"

"Mothers know these things. Would you like a cookie?"

She was a big woman, pudgy, her chubby round cheeks crowding her eyes so that she always seemed to be squinting. She was built big for hugging, Vera liked to say, and she hugged Andy often. Ben harbored a jealousy he couldn't name, wouldn't admit. His memories of his own mother were dear and few — one in particular: a pretty woman, wisps of brown hair sticking out from under a yellow bathing cap, singing softly; sand in his shoes, sunshine in his eyes. Whether it was a memory from the day she drowned, he didn't know.

The air in Vera's cottage was heavy with a sweet, damp aroma. She went into the kitchen and returned bearing a tray with a plate full of cookies, a jug of milk and two glasses. "I baked these today," she said. Setting the tray on the coffee table, she motioned for Ben to sit on the sofa, upholstered in a bright gold and white floral design, and put another stick on the fire in the fireplace. Ben's mouth was watering. He'd never visited Aunt Vera by himself. He'd always been with Andy.

She sat on the end of the sofa closest to the fire, leaving enough room between them for another person to sit. A small person. Andy would have fit perfectly.

"Help yourself," she said. Ben didn't have to be told twice. The aroma had made him hungry. They ate. They watched the fire. "What happened to him?" Ben said.

Vera kept staring at the dancing flames. "Something," she said to the fire.

It occurred to Ben this was something he'd known all along.

"Did you know he loved to have his back tickled?" Vera looked over at Ben just as he was stuffing the last of his fourth cookie into his mouth. "Did he ever tell you?" Ben couldn't answer, his mouth so full. He shook his head no.

"Oh, how that boy loved back tickles." She looked again at the fire, cookie crumbs on her bosom and on her lap, on her green, embroidered dressing gown. "He would get on his knees, right here," Vera pointed at the rug by her feet, "and take off his shirt and lay across my lap and I would tickle his back, very lightly, all over, with my fingernails. That's why I kept them so long, just for Andy's back tickles."

The back tickles struck Ben as fodder that could be useful for teasing Andy. But then it occurred to him. The way Vera was talking about him. In the past tense.

"You never saw such goosebumps." Vera looked at her fingernails. A tear rolled down her chubby cheek. "I suppose I can cut them now."

WHEN ALL THE SEARCHING turned up nothing, they searched again. The creek was dragged again, upstream and down. The wooded areas of town, the hills and woods in every direction, were scoured by search parties, more than once, some places more than twice. The State Police brought in dogs, to no avail.

No one swam in the swimming hole. The boys who'd been there Sunday afternoon kept to themselves, gathering only in two's or three's, half-heartedly playing their games, marbles, mumblety-peg, always speaking of Andy: Andy's whereabouts, the odds he was still alive, the chances they'd be blamed for whatever ill fate had befallen him, their degree of blame after what had happened that afternoon at the swimming hole. Darryl and Jack, the two boys who'd thrown Andy into the drink, were conspicuously inconspicuous.

It wasn't all grave. Andy had probably caught poison ivy on his bare bum and scratched himself to death. A bear had eaten him and his parents were waiting for it to shit out his remains for burial. A hawk had mistaken him for a skinny, bald rat and carried him off in its clutches to the wilds of northern Canada.

His clothes were found. His pants turned up along the bank of the creek a few hundred yards upstream, his sweater behind a rhododendron in a vacant lot halfway across town, his underpants in a mailbox on Jefferson Street.

But the boy himself remained missing.

Harry Clinger — his uncle, with whom Andy lived, and who a few still believed was his real father — joined the searches, his eyes red and swollen. A gentle man nearly sixty, he was not in the best of shape, somewhat portly, and some wondered if his bereavement over the fate of his nephew might have resulted from a guilty conscious.

Harry's wife Frances remained at home minding her garden, seemingly indifferent, as if she didn't care if the boy — her stepson, if he was anything to her — was ever found or not. Childless herself, she was known to have resented having to raise Andy as her own, generating suspicions galore.

Andy's real mother, "Aunt" Vera, was generally above suspicion, though there were those who thought perhaps she was just unhinged enough to have done something crazy.

Vera carried on with her normal routine, showing up at the church thrift shop on Pershing Street, just around the corner from Main, every morning at nine, dutifully keeping track of stock, meager though it was, handling sales, meager though they were, while steadily crafting her own contributions, crafting her famous reindeer out of clothespins and yarn. Nearly every customer, of whom there were few, mentioned Andy, what a pity, what a shame.

Vera tisked aloud, shook her head, and said God's will be done.

She flipped the sign on the thrift shop door to "Closed" at three o'clock on Friday afternoon, shut and locked the door with a jangle of bells, dodged Mrs. Seibert on the sidewalk as she stepped out, commencing her long walk home as though she were wearing blinders. The large woman strode steadily down Main Street, back straight, her chin up. It was the finest day of the year so far, late May, cloudless and warm. Five days since Andy had disappeared. Vera kept her cardigan on despite the annoying trickles of sweat rolling down her skin beneath her plain, black-and-yellow dress. She was about to cross Main Street when Mr. Radaker came by in his automobile, coughing and spewing fumes, and Vera had to wait until the coast was clear. She didn't entirely approve of automobiles. But then she supposed no one cared what she approved of or didn't. She made her way along Franklin, passing within spitting distance of Ben's and Andy's clubhouse (of which she was unaware), and continued up the hill, past the imposing brick school house with its towering turrets. Reaching home, she walked up the path to her little porch but didn't go inside. She sat in the worn wicker rocking chair, the only chair on the porch, beside the tall clay planter with the dead stalks sticking up.

Shortly, she walked back out to the picket fence. She stooped to pluck a particularly fat yellow dandelion, sniffed at it, sneezed it, dropped it, and continued down the road toward the Clinger's. When she got there, she paused to take it in: the sprawling, well-trimmed, dandelion-free lawn, the rambling, mustard-yellow house with green shutters and trim, the gables and mansards, and behind the house the little barn where Harry had kept his horse when he had one, which he hadn't for several years. There was a loft in the little barn.

She walked up to the steps, across the porch and into the house without knocking. Harry and Frances stood in the kitchen, facing off, faces flushed from arguing. They looked at her.

"They haven't found him yet, have they?"

"No, Vera," Harry said to his younger sister. "Don't you think I'd have told you?"

"Has anyone looked in the barn? The barn out back?"

"Yes. That's been searched." Frances was curt. She had no time for Vera. Never had.

"They've looked everywhere." Harry jingled a handful of coins in his pocket.

"They didn't look in that loft." Vera turned, heading for the back door.

"Now hold on," Frances said in an unkind tone.

Harry said, "They did. Of course they did."

Vera opened the door and was gone. Harry and Frances, exchanging glances, followed.

In the shadows inside the barn rested an old wagon, alongside assorted tack and other rusting implements, smelling of mildew and mud and musty straw. Vera quickly glanced around the interior as the others followed her into the shadows. She made for the ladder to the loft and began to climb, her weight challenging the rungs.

"Vera!" Harry went after her.

"Come back down here, you stupid woman!" said Frances.

'Harry followed her up the ladder.

In the loft were the cobwebs, dust and detritus of half a century. And a box. A small wooden storage box. Vera stopped short, looking over the box. Harry did as well. Frances remained downstairs. The silence lasted a few seconds, nothing but a random creak from the old barn's timbers, and the beating of the wings of a large bird flying just beyond the loft window. From down below came Frances's scream, "No! No! No!" followed by sobs. Vera turned away. Harry approached the box, knelt, flipped the latches and opened it.

And thus was Andy found.

THERE'D BEEN MURDERS BEFORE in Hartsgrove, but never one like this. Never before a child. Never one so filled with juicy mystery, so utterly lacking a prime suspect. Over the past hundred years, husbands had killed wives, wives had killed husbands, acquaintances had killed one another. Most could be blamed on demon rum. One of the most notorious had occurred a scant fifty years before when two young men — strangers from another place — had conspired to rob an old widow named Betsy McCullough under the guise of looking for work. During the course of the robbery, Betsy was struck on the head with a mallet and murdered; one of the men, Thomas McAfoose, had been caught. The other escaped. McAfoose was the last person to be publicly executed in the yard of the Hartsgrove Courthouse. Hundreds had watched the spectacle of his hanging.

When the new day dawned, it dawned on a new town. Word had leaked out and spread, like a poisonous gas. The air was rife with shock, grief and suspicion. Never before had a murder so senseless and seemingly insoluble cast its shadow over the town. When neighbor spoke to neighbor, when friends and acquaintances came together on Main Street, the murder of the child was the first thing on their lips. He'd been found in a storage box, bent over double to fit; he was naked except for a pair of underpants, a pair that were much too large; he was wet, though he had not drowned. There were marks on his throat, bruises on his head.

Who could do such a thing? When neighbor spoke to neighbor, when friend spoke to friend, it was with a new degree of wonder and suspicion as they tried to see into the eyes of the other person, tried to see through the eyes and into the very soul: Was this person capable of taking a life into his hands and slowly, deliberately, methodically extinguishing it? Taking away the very existence of a fellow human being?

———

THE FIREFLIES WERE GLORIOUS. Vera sat in the worn wicker rocker on her small front porch, Ben close by, sitting next to the planter with the dead stalks sticking up. After sunset, a warm evening, the fireflies were out in profusion, lighting up her yard just as a million stars lighted the dark heavens. The soft, warm, amber blinking was a balm, mesmerizing, and both Vera and Ben sat for some minutes in silence, the only sound the far-off barking of a dog somewhere across town, the odd cry of an owl from the woods behind the house.

It had been over a week since Andy was found.

Vera reached down and took Ben's hand. "Will you be my little boy now?"

Ben looked up, surprised and confused, warmth creeping over him. He'd come to visit Vera to escape the loneliness of his house. He almost hadn't; he'd had to work up his courage, overcome his shyness. He wanted to talk about his friend, Andy. He wanted to feel, however vicariously, the comfort of a warm, loving mother.

When the first mosquito struck, they went inside. They sat on the sofa eating cookies, sipping milk. They started a fire. Talked about Andy. Tears came again to Vera's eyes and Ben looked away, fearful of crying himself.

"He didn't seem to be a very happy boy," Vera said. "Did he?"

Ben hadn't thought of it that way. "He told me everybody hated him."

Vera flinched. "Did you tell him *I* loved him?"

"Yes," Ben lied. "I told him lots of folks loved him."

What Ben didn't say, what Vera didn't say was this: *Who could have done such a thing?* The speculation that was rife all over town had no place in Vera's little living room. Hundreds of other conversations had soaked that ground; any more would simply run off, like rain off a saturated field.

Ben's father and Andy's stepmother Frances had been caught by Andy in a compromising moment; they had to make sure he wouldn't tell his uncle, Harry. Or did Andy tell? And did Harry, shocked and distraught, overreact and kill the messenger? Why was the boy wet? Had he been hidden in one of the Clingers' rain barrels until he was moved to the box in the loft? Who could have done that? Who else but Harry? Or Frances.

A shell-shocked soldier, Johnny Haskell, had been sent home from the war, and he lived near the creek where he often fished, and often lost his temper when the boys taunted him, splashing the water, scaring the fish. Who knows what Haskell might have done? Some of the bigger, rougher boys wanted to ensure that Andy didn't squeal. Things had gotten out of hand. Maybe it was an accident. A hobo, a pervert, had come across the nearly naked boy.

And Vera herself. How had she known that something had happened to him?

Mothers know those things. Mothers feel those things.

Vera and Ben stared at the fire, as mesmerized as they had been by the fireflies. When Vera finally spoke again, she said, "Do you think he's in a better place now?"

Ben ceased chewing, suddenly ashamed of his overstuffed mouthful of cookies. He brushed a crumb from the corner of his lip and swallowed, looking at Vera, at her round face and fat cheeks and green squinted eyes. "I don't know... If he's up in heaven. I guess so."

"If he's any place but here. It's not called a vale of tears for nothing. It has to be a better place. Look all around you. All those millions of young men getting killed over there in that horrible war that maims what it doesn't kill. Just look at poor Johnny Haskell. And what's left are dying by that, that disease, that flu — that *Spanish* Flu. And it's here now. It's on its way to Hartsgrove. It's a plague. God is punishing us. We're sinners, all of us, poor sinners. I'm *glad* Andy's not here. He's free and at peace now. He doesn't have to suffer anymore."

Ben blinked like a kitten. He wasn't sure what to think. Andy would never be able to swim or fish again, never be able to run through the field, never play baseball, never be able to lie on his back and look up at the clouds in the sky. Never meet in their clubhouse, plan and plot and laugh. Ben only nodded and took another surreptitious nibble of cookie.

"Would you like me to tickle your back? Like I used to tickle Andy's?"

Ben froze in mid-nibble, hesitant. He snapped at the lure.

Pulling off his T-shirt, he knelt on the throw rug, lay across Vera's lap. "Like this?" he said. When she began running her fingernails lightly over the skin of his back, Ben felt a sensation so pleasurable it took his breath away. A cascade of goosebumps overtook his body, not just his back, but his arms, his legs, every square inch of his skin. He couldn't believe how good it felt. He moaned in pleasure.

Vera said, "Like that."

Ben was at the mercy of waves of pleasure that left him speechless. But it was more. It was a mother. *So this is what it means to have a mother.*

"Andy doesn't have to be afraid anymore," Vera cooed, sing-song, as if to a baby. "No more mean boys stealing all his clothes, no more mean boys throwing him in the water."

She stopped for a moment, then resumed the light work of her tickling fingers. Loving fingers. A mother's fingers. "But you were there for him, weren't you, Benny? Benny, good Benny. Giving him your very own underpants. Such a generous thing to do. Good Benny."

Ben flinched. His underpants? More goosebumps emerged, goosebumps upon goosebumps, but now they were from an entirely different place, of an entirely different color. No one knew where Andy's oversized underpants had come from but him and Andy.

So this is what it means to have a mother.

—THE END—

About the Author

The late Dennis McFadden, a retired project manager, lived and wrote in a cedar-shingled cottage called Summerhill in the woods of upstate New York. His first short fiction collection, *Hart's Grove,* was published by Colgate University Press in 2010, and his second, *Jimtown Road,* won the 2016 Press 53 Award for Short Fiction; another collection, *Lafferty, Looking for Love,* is forthcoming from Cornerstone Press. His novel, *Old Grimes Is Dead,* earned a starred review from Kirkus Reviews, and was selected by their editors as one of the Best Indie Books of 2022. Over a hundred of his stories have appeared in publications such as *The Missouri Review, New England Review, The Sewanee Review, Arts & Letters, The Antioch Review, Crazyhorse, The Massachusetts Review, Ellery Queen Mystery Magazine, Alfred Hitchcock Mystery Magazine, The Best American Mystery Stories* (three times) and in the 2021 inaugural volume of *The Best Mystery Stories of the Year* series. A Pushcart Prize nominee, he also frequently served as the judge of *Prime Number Magazine*'s Short Fiction Award, and as their guest short fiction editor.

The Nightingale Sings No More

By Gary R. Bush

1936 WAS ANOTHER YEAR of heat and drought. Dust blew in from the open window. The oppressive heat and noise from traffic on Seven Corners was getting on my nerves. The block of ice in front of my fan was melting faster than Jesse Owens running the 100-meter dash and yesterday's St. Paul *Daily News* headline had announced that the heat killed 100 people in the Twin Cities. Farmers were demanding Governor Olson get them some relief. But Floyd B. Olson was in the Mayo Clinic dying of stomach cancer.

We all had our problems. I hadn't had a client in more than a month. A nice divorce case would be swell, but none of the lawyers I knew were throwing business my way. If I had the energy, I'd go to the drugstore and get a Coke. Then the phone rang and startled me out of my sulk. I answered on the second ring. "O'Connell Investigations, Michael O'Connell speaking."

"Mr. O'Connell, my name is Margot Enright. I wonder if I could prevail on you to come to my residence to discuss a rather delicate matter?" There was a slight tremor in her voice. "Of course, I shall pay you for your time. Do you suppose you could be here within the hour?"

"Certainly, Miss Enright."

She gave her address on Summit Avenue and hung up.

Margot Enright was not unknown to me. She was a famous painter of children's portraits. She was also the heir to the Enright timber, mining, and railroad fortune. Her engagement to William Yarbury — the attorney soon to be a State Supreme Court justice — was in all the papers. I knew Yarbury, having worked for him last year.

I grabbed my linen jacket, straightened my tie, set my Panama hat at a jaunty angle, and went down and caught the streetcar on the corner. I could have walked, but it was too damn hot to attempt Summit Hill. I moved to the open back of the car, hoping to catch a breath of air.

I transferred to the Selby line and rode through the tunnel that had been cut through St. Anthony Hill so that the streetcars could make the grade. At the Cathedral of St. Paul, I hopped off where Selby crosses Summit. I strolled up Summit, until I came to the red sandstone and brick castle that was the Enright mansion. I wiped the back of my neck with my already soaked handkerchief and rang the bell.

A maid answered the door. The top of her head, covered in strawberry blonde curls, barely reached my chin, and judging by her pose, with her arms on her hips and the frown on her face, she didn't look pleased to see me. Despite her frown, she was pretty as a fine day in spring. She gave me the once-over and said in not too friendly a manner, "You must be the copper Miss Enright be expectin'." Her lilt came straight from the Auld Sod.

Putting on my own brogue, "Sure now, that's no way to be treatin' a fella from Dublin's fair city."

"I don't like coppers, Irish, English or Yanks."

"How about ex-coppers, Miss..."

"O'Shea, if you must know." She gave me a little smile. "But I take no blarney, ex-cop or not. So mind your manners."

"As if I was sittin' church. Would your first name be Rick?"

She stopped for a minute. "Rick O'Shea? Ricochet!" She burst out laughing. "Since you inquired, it's Riona."

"A queenly name for a queenly woman."

"I told you, no blarney. I'll take your hat and show you to Miss Enright. She's in her tower studio. Now, would you ride the lift, or are you strong enough to take the stairs?"

"The stairs, if it allows me to spend more time with you."

She elbowed me in the ribs. "I said, 'no blarney.'"

I liked this girl, but I was here for a job, so we rode the lift after all.

Before we got off, she warned me. "You be nice to Miss Enright or, ex-copper or not, I'll make yer life a livin' hell." And with that, she led me to the studio.

"That *detective* is here, miss."

"Thank you, Riona. Could you please bring up a pitcher of lemonade?"

Miss Enright turned to me. "Would you prefer something stronger, Mr. O'Connell?"

I shook my head. The gift of gab eluded me — and me a son of Ireland. I had only seen her photos in the newspapers, and knew she was an attractive woman, but I was really stunned by her beauty. Even wearing an artist's smock and with a smear of blue paint on her left cheek, she would put many Hollywood actresses to shame. Her dark hair framed a heart-shaped face, her skin was a pale white, and she had the most startling blue eyes I had ever seen. Five years older than I, she looked ten years younger.

Miss Enright flashed a beautiful smile and led me to a low table by the window, where there was a magnificent view of the Mississippi, the High Bridge, and Cherokee Heights. She covered a painting she was working on, wiped her brush, and set it in turpentine.

Riona returned with the lemonade. "Do you want me stay, Miss?" she asked, setting the tray on the table.

"That won't be necessary," she said.

Riona reluctantly left, but not before giving me a warning look.

"That's some bodyguard you've got there," I said, picking up my glass.

She smiled. "Riona's loyal, and truth be told, she has my confidence in the matter I wish to discuss."

I waited for her to continue.

"Last year you worked for my fiancée, William Yarbury, on a child custody case."

I nodded. Yarbury was a lawyer who had hired me to investigate an old money financier who had married an attractive shop girl named Doris Clark. A girl shall we say, "not of his class." They had a child, a boy. Baggett divorced her after the boy was born. He claimed Doris was an unfit mother and demanded custody. Yarbury represented Doris and hired me to look into Baggett. I found enough evidence to prove he was a philanderer and a gambler, and had on several occasions bilked his clients.

"I hate bullies. And too many women lose custody to men like Baggett. It was one case I enjoyed working on," I explained.

"William once said you were one of the few honest policemen in St. Paul."

"Well, he was kind to say so, but that's not exactly true. I looked the other way more than once." *And took my share of bribes.* St. Paul was infamous for the O'Conner System. Beginning in 1900, then-chief of police, John O'Connor, allowed criminals to stay in the city under three conditions: that they checked in with police when they arrived; agreed to pay bribes to city officials; and committed no major crimes in the city of St. Paul. It only ended a year ago, when the newspapers exposed the racket.

"But you resigned from the department," Miss Enright said.

"Only after I found out that the former chief had his hand in kidnapping of the brewery heir, William Hamm, Jr. There are crimes I hate, including kidnapping, murder, and blackmail. And guys like Baggett."

Miss Enright nodded. "I believe you are the right man for the job." She took a deep breath. "I'm being blackmailed. I need you to find the person or persons and retrieve items that are being used against me." She took a sip of her lemonade.

"It's a rather long story," she continued. "I was studying painting in New York when the war started. I joined the Red Cross and was sent to France." She handed me a photo of a group of women in Red Cross uniforms. I spotted her right away.

"I served as a nurse at the American Red Cross Military Hospital No. 1, west of Paris, at Neuilly-sur-Seine."

I held up my hand. "I was a patient there. Wounded at Belleau Wood."

Her eyes widened. "I was there when they brought in you Marines."

"Your people saved my life."

She smiled and went on. "After the war, I stayed in Paris to continue my studies. I met an artist, Lucien Chatel. We fell in love and I became his model as well as his pupil. I'm not ashamed to say I posed nude. The painting is not the problem, it's the photographs."

"Photographs?"

She nodded. "Lucien used a camera to establish poses. Some were full nudes." She shrugged as if it didn't matter.

"Poor Lucien died of the flu in '22. Heartbroken, I left for home and took the portrait and the photos with me. The painting is now in my bedroom. But when I opened the packet of pictures, I noticed two of the photos were missing. Yesterday I received this letter."

She handed me the letter. It was postmarked Minneapolis. The letter was printed on cheap lined paper, with several spelling errors.

PAY $50 THOSAND IN UNMARKED BILLS OR
OTHER PICTUR WILL BE SENT TO GOVENER AND
NEWSPAPERS. WAIT FERTHER INSTRUTIONS.
NO COPS.

She took a deep breath. "I couldn't care less about my reputation. I have money and my art and I can return to France. It's William I worry about. He is about to be named to the State Supreme Court, and the scandal will kill his chances."

"If those two photos weren't with the others, they must have been stolen in France," I said. "Someone who knew you then and is probably here, has them. Perhaps it was one of the women you served with who stayed on after the war."

"I can't believe that," she said. "Those women were like sisters. Many came from fine families. None would think of such a thing. Besides, the writer is nearly illiterate."

"Maybe someone just wanted you to think that. Money is always a motive. With the Depression in full swing, many people are in dire straits. You've weathered the crash, others aren't so lucky."

"If any of those girls needed money, all they had to do was ask. No, what you say is impossible."

"Some people are too proud or too ashamed to beg." I picked up the picture of her and the Red Cross women.

"Can you account for these women and their whereabouts?" I asked.

She took the photo from me. She pointed to three women. "They were all killed in the war." Tears formed in her eyes, and she dabbed them with her handkerchief.

She eliminated them one by one. Five were married and well off. Two were still in France and lived together as lovers. They had money. Three were still living in Minnesota. Others were scattered across the country. Two, she had no idea where they were.

I picked up the picture and pointed to one of the women she had lost track of, a very attractive blonde. "She's familiar, who is she?"

"That's Oletta Earnshaw. She was the youngest of us. I think she lied about her age. I last saw her in September 1921. It was at a birthday party for the artist Suzanne Valadon. Oletta said she was going home, that she'd had enough of Paris and 'the so-called Bohemian life.' I never saw her leave the party. I heard she had gone to New York."

She sat back in her chair. "Perhaps you remember her from the hospital? She was a canteen girl. As lovely as she was, many of the patients were enamored of her."

"My eyes were bandaged due to my wound."

"It couldn't be her. She sang for you boys, held your hands."

"The Nightingale!" I said. "I remember she sang, *There's a Long, Long Trail A-Winding*. I never heard a voice so pure."

She nodded. "The voice of an angel."

"Yes," I said.

She had stopped crying. "Now what?"

"Wait for the instructions and notify me. I'll take it from there."

"Should I gather the money?"

"Yes, in case you're being watched."

I stood up and we shook hands. She rang for Riona. While we waited, she asked me, "Do you have a car?"

"No, I use the streetcar and taxis or hire a car when I need one."

"My Packard is at your disposal. Riona can give you the keys."

"If I parked a Packard in Seven Corners, it would be gone or stripped as soon as sundown."

"If you need a car, I'll send Riona to pick you up. Just call."

"She can drive?"

"As well as any bloke, and better than most."

Riona piped up. I hadn't seen her enter the room. "Miss Enright and I took lessons from Tommy Milton, the famous race car driver."

I couldn't help but smile. "Not Eddie Rickenbacker?"

"Eddie wasn't available," Miss Enright said, in all seriousness. "Riona, would you be kind enough to drive Mr. O'Connell downtown? Oh, and show him my portrait."

"If I must," she said, but I saw the twinkle in her eye.

The portrait was tasteful. She was draped in silk, with just a suggestion of breasts and well-shaped legs. Lucien had captured her face and those eyes to perfection. I've seen women showing more and with less class at the Boulevards of Paris nightclub on Lexington Parkway.

"Well, if you're done gawkin'," Riona said to me, "I'll run you home."

The car was a silver-colored Packard Twelve Sports Phaeton. "Where to?"

"The Moore Building."

She fired up the engine and we went flying down Summit. She drove like she was at the Indy 500. I just held on to my hat and hoped for the best.

"Why do you hate cops?" I asked when we reached my building and she had parked in front.

"They killed me own da, him not even in the IRA. Then my ma died of a broken heart.

"So, I come to America with me older sister, Deirdre. She puts me in a convent school and goes to work for some swell. He rapes her and she goes to the cops and they turn her away. She winds up on the streets and is beaten and killed by some pimp. The peelers don't give a damn." Tears streamed down her cheeks.

Deirdre an Bhrói, I thought to myself, remembering the Irish myth — Deirdre of the sorrows.

I wrapped my arms around her and held her until her sobs subsided.

She wiped her tears, took a deep breath and nodded. "So now you know. Miss Enright heard about my situation and rescued me from the school after there was no money to pay them."

"I came over at twelve, an orphan, too," I said. "But my uncle Dion and Aunt Moira took me in. Dion was a cop and after I came back from the war, he got me on the force. And now you know my story."

"Only some of it," she said, hinting she wanted to hear more.

I took her hand, "If you're okay to drive, I'll get to work on the case."

"I'll be fine, now that I got that off my chest."

"What was the name of the pimp who killed your sister?"

"I'll never forget. Grady Fry."

I nodded. He was still around.

"And the man who raped her?"

"Killed himself after the crash in '29." She sniffed.

THE FAN WAS STILL blowing, but the ice block I had put beneath it had melted. I dumped the bucket, sat back, and began to think. The name and face of Oletta Earnshaw, the attractive blonde in the photo of the nurses who had looked familiar, kept popping into my head. Where had I seen her? I paced around my office, but the harder I tried, the less I could remember. I'd just have to wait for the blackmailer to contact Miss Enright and go from there.

I planned to have a talk with Grady Fry when this case was closed. Fry was a snake who palled around with other snakes — thieves, pimps dope dealers... *dope dealers.* That was it. Fry had a pal, Cal Dyer. Dyer was a dope dealer, heroin mostly. Saw him a few years back with a beautiful woman he called Letty. Good God! Letty was Oletta Earnshaw.

Fry was going to lead me to Dyer. Who might lead me to Oletta.

FRY HUNG OUT AT the Coliseum Ballroom next to the Boulevards of Paris, where he recruited young girls.

I took my 1903 Colt .32 Auto. It was only six inches long and easy to conceal.

I waited until ten that evening, then grabbed a cab to the Coliseum at Lexington and University Avenue. It was easy to spot Fry. He stood by the door, eyeing all the women without escorts. He was dressed in a well-tailored suit, his dark hair slicked back, and the pencil-thin mustache on his handsome face gave him the appearance of a lead actor in a B-movie. He was talking to a young blonde, probably fresh off the farm.

"So," he said to her. "I saw you dancing out there. You remind me of Ginger Rogers. I think you could be a professional. I can get you an audition."

She giggled. "Really?"

"The only audition he'll get you is one on your back. Run away, girl, if you want to save yourself from prostitution," I interrupted.

She turned bright red and actually did run away across the ballroom.

"O'Connell, you son-of-a-bitch, you ain't a cop no more." He cocked his fist, and that's when I jabbed him in the ribs with the Colt.

He blanched white as I steered him out to the parking lot. "Where's your car?" He pointed to a new Buick Roadmaster.

"Pimping must be good business," I said forcing him into the driver's seat sliding in next to him.

"What the hell's this about?" He tried to sound tough, but his voice was shaking. "I want you to take me to your pal, Cal Dyer."

"That's all? You could have asked politely."

I jabbed him with the gun. "Shut up and drive."

"He lives in South St. Paul off of Concord."

We headed east on University to Highway 56 and crossed the river. The stink of the stockyards permeated the air.

"Do you remember a girlfriend of his, Letty something?" I asked.

"Yeah, she's still with him."

He pulled up in front of an apartment building. "Cal owns the place. Can I go now?" Fry asked.

"No, you're going in."

He didn't argue. He remembered my gun.

Dyer lived on the second floor. Fry pressed the buzzer. "Yeah?" someone said.

"Cal, it's me. Grady."

"Christ, it's midnight. I suppose you wanna stash one of your broads here."

I poked him. "Yeah," he mumbled.

Dyer buzzed us in and when we reached his door, Fry knocked. When Dyer opened up, I shoved Fry forward hard enough to knock Dyer down.

"What the..." Dyer's voice failed when he saw my gun.

"Stay on the floor, and Fry, you sit next to him. Either one of you make a move, I shoot."

"Dyer, where's Letty?" I asked.

"Bedroom."

"Call her."

"Letty, get out here."

She came out of the bedroom. Thin as a wraith, with dark circles under her eyes, hair uncombed. It took me a minute to realize this was the same Oletta Earnshaw, the one in the photograph and the beautiful girl I'd seen with Dyer only two years ago.She looked at me with eyes that were the same as the shell-shocked boys I'd known in the war.

"Oletta," I whispered.

"No one's called me that in years. Do I know you?"

"From France, Nightingale." When I said France, she broke down in tears, and it all came tumbling out.

"I was good then. I tried to help. But it was too heartbreaking. Those broken boys without limbs, without faces. I held their hands, I sang for them, and they died. Morphine for them, morphine for me. After the war I tried to forget. I went wild in Paris. I drank, I took more drugs. The memories..."

She sobbed. "I came home but nothing was the same. *Flaming youth* they called us. I burned out fast." She gave a frenzied laugh. "Those two came into my life." She pointed to Fry. "He tried to turn me out. But Cal wanted to *save* me. He saved me to be his own whore. Just gave me the needle when I needed it. I was his eye candy, but no more."

Dyer looked as if he was about to say something, but shut up fast when I pointed my gun at him.

"Tell me about the pictures," I asked Oletta gently.

"I found them one day. I meant no harm, Margot was so daring. I just took them, I don't even know why." She shrugged. "Cal found the pictures a week ago and recognized Margot from the papers. I would never use them against her. His rotten idea."

"Shut your goddamn mouth!" Dyer yelled. "I'll kick the living shit out of you."

I smacked him hard. "You'll never touch her again."

"Oletta, "I said in a quiet voice, "please bring me the pictures and any copies."

She nodded and brought the pictures. I refused to look at them.

"Can I go now?" Fry pleaded. "I done what you asked."

"Fry, do you remember Deirdre O'Shea? An Irish girl new to America?" He probably didn't remember Riona's sister, Deirdre, but I was going to try anyway.

"Huh? Yeah, she's dead."

"You killed her."

"An accident, I swear. She wanted to send money to some convent school for her sister. I said her sister could live with me. She went nuts, attacked me. It was self-defense."

"You beat her to death." The wild look in my eyes shook him.

I tied the hands of both men with lamp cord, and gagged them. "Oletta, I'm taking them out of here. I'll come back for you. I'll get you help, I promise."

She gave me a pathetic smile, but I'm not sure she heard me. I marched the men to the car and forced them into the trunk. I heard their muffled curses all the way to the railyard by the stockyards. I rolled them out of the trunk, picked up the tire iron, and shoved them toward the stock cars waiting to be unloaded in the morning. At a car full of hogs, I broke the lock. Wide-eyed, the two began to shake. I removed their gags.

"What are you going to do?" Dyer whined.

"Neither of you are fit to sleep with pigs," I told him. "But you're going to die with them. Fry, you murdered a woman and used so many more. Dyer, your drugs ruined lives and you broke a damaged Nightingale."

"Nightingale? Who the f..." That's when I cracked his jaw with the iron. I did the same to Fry a second later. They were both alive and bleeding, when I heaved them in with the pigs and slammed the door. I tried to ignore the cries and the squealing as I walked away.

I drove back to the apartment and found Oletta lying on the floor with a needle in her arm. She was still alive, barely. I kneeled beside her. "Oletta, it'll be all right. I'll get you help."

"No help for the wicked," she whispered.

"You were never wicked. You saw too much suffering in your young life. The war did this to you, as much as it did to the boys you nurtured."

I sang to her, as once she sang to me.

> *"There's a long, long trail a-winding*
> *Into the land of my dreams,*
> *Where the nightingales are singing*
> *And the white moon beams*
> *There's a long, long night of waiting*
> *Until all my dreams come true;*
> *Till the day I'll be going down*
> *That long, long trail with you."*

She smiled and took her last breath. I picked her up and laid her on the bed. The Nightingale of Neuily-sur-Seine was gone.

I made an anonymous call to the cops, and told them where she was. The next day I told Margot and Riona some of what had happened. The *Pioneer Press* reported the deaths of Dyer and Fry. The police chalked it up to rival criminals.

Margot arranged a funeral for Oletta. I went, of course.

Margot and William had a small but elegant wedding. I attended with Riona on my arm.

—THE END—

About the Author

A historian by training, Gary R. Bush writes fiction for adults, young adults, and children. He is co-editor of the anthology *Once Upon a Crime*, a collection of short stories from some of the world's best mystery authors. His stories have appeared in numerous anthologies. Bush is also the award-winning author of the YA novel, *Jamie Sharpe and the Seas of Treachery*, which is followed by *Jamie Sharpe and the Pirates of Barbary*, as well as a novella prequel, *Jamie Sharpe and the Voyage to Hell's Island*. By fall of 2026, look for *Jamie Sharpe and the Journey to Hostile Shores*. Away from writing, Bush enjoys sailing and has sailed on the Atlantic, Pacific, and Lake Superior. He has always loved stories of adventure and the sea. Bush lives in Minneapolis with his journalist wife, Stacey.

The School Girl and The Illusionist

By C. C. Guthrie

"Mr. Amon Carter will rue the day he hired a stripper to perform at the Fort Worth Frontier Centennial Show," Myrna Hofmann said. She was a faithful front-pew churchgoer who was in hog heaven when she lectured others on right and wrong. "Watching a show called Sally Rand's Nude Ranch is not how decent folks should celebrate the one-hundredth anniversary of Texas's independence."

For once, Myrna's hissy fit wasn't directed at me, so I joined the conversation. "Mr. Carter's paper said Sally Rand's act is an illusion. She only looks naked because she wears a skin-colored costume and is hidden behind fans, bubbles, and balloons on stage."

Big mistake.

Myrna's head snapped in my direction faster than a rattlesnake went for a bunny. "Lillian Caufield, a fifteen-year-old girl should not be part of this conversation. Especially one who doesn't own dresses that properly cover her legs."

As if I could have stopped growing.

"Sally Rand is not a stripper," Wendell Rosales said. Rosie, as he was known, was the chief mechanic for the biggest airline at Fort Worth's Meacham Field. He was used to being in charge and didn't like it when people argued with him. "Sally Rand was the star of the World's Fair in '33. If her show was fine three years ago, why isn't it now?"

Myrna sniffed. "Because that was Chicago, and this is Fort Worth. But even they arrested her four times in one day."

"But she wasn't naked," Rosie said. "So, they allowed her to continue performing."

Just when it seemed like the argument would go on all afternoon, Myrna's boss, the Meacham Field manager, waved his arms. "Listen up, now. The flight just left Dallas and should be here directly."

Nothing made that man happier than an on-time airplane. With a big smile and outstretched arms, he preached about the future of aviation like a pastor talked about the pearly gates. As long as the conversation involved airplanes, he'd talk to an oil-covered wildcatter or one of the Roosevelts in town to visit the President's son. Folks surged forward and knotted up around him in front of the open terminal window. I stayed put. The Texas heat had barely started, so I wasn't going to sweat before I had to.

Although everyone in the terminal worked at Meacham, they acted like they'd never seen a celebrity before. I had, and I only sold bottles of Dr Pepper and my pimento cheese sandwiches after school, on weekends, and during summer vacation.

While everyone else in the terminal chattered about Sally Rand's arrival, I tidied up my workspace because my day was over. As soon as Sally arrived, Mr. Carter's driver would whisk her downtown, where she'd be treated to a bigshot welcome.

As I slipped my clean sandwich knife into my pocket, Calvin Grzesk turned away from the terminal window and bounced up and down like he'd just won his first game of marbles. In a voice that quivered with excitement, he shouted, "It's here."

He was a full-fledged mechanical genius who didn't give a hoot about Sally Rand. All he wanted to see was the brand spanking new DC-3 bringing her into town. Last month, he'd graduated from high school one day and reported to Rosie the next as an airplane repair apprentice.

I edged up to the window as the sun glinted off the silver bird's wings when it lined up for landing. It briefly disappeared behind a cloud, then dipped down to kiss the runway. Everyone else in the terminal was impressed, too. They responded to the perfect landing with cheers, claps, and whistles. I couldn't wait until I learned how to do that. The shiny plane passed the terminal, made a wide turn, and rolled to a stop outside our window.

After Calvin called out, "Propellers off, door open, stairs down," he rushed out to chock the wheels and was back inside in less than a minute.

A smiling stewardess appeared in the doorway. She waved to the two ground handlers who wheeled mail and luggage carts across the tarmac for the cargo they'd unload on the other side of the plane. Then she stepped back, and another woman took her place in the opening.

"Is that Sally Rand?" The Braniff Air Lines ticket agent shrieked with emotion, her question echoing through the waiting area.

The passenger, in no hurry to leave the airplane, slowly scanned the ramp.

"What's she waiting for?" someone asked. "Why isn't she getting off?"

The cargo handlers emerged from the other side of the plane, pushing nearly empty carts. The woman followed their progress across the tarmac, her head moving from left to right as the employees approached the operations hangar next to the cabbie area, where two men stood.

I knew all the drivers and I'd never seen those two. They wore flashy suits and hats that no Fort Worth man would have worn on a hundred-dollar bet.

The taller fella held up a sign with Sally Rand's name printed on it. The woman ignored him and shifted her gaze to the terminal window where we gawked. She smiled at us, then stepped back and disappeared into the plane.

"Maybe that's not her," a voice in the crowd said. "After all, there isn't a Star-Telegram reporter or photographer here to meet the plane."

"The only name on the Dallas passenger manifest is Sally Rand," the ticket agent said in a snippy tone.

With nothing to do but stare at an airplane that wasn't going anywhere, folks began to fidget in the overheated terminal. One by one, women unsnapped pocketbooks and pulled out Crosby Funeral Home fans. Not that their flapping cooled us down. All it did was move around the hot air and stir up the cigarette smoke and dust.

When a new face appeared in the airplane's doorway, Calvin was the first to spot the four stripes on the man's jacket cuff and announced, "He's the airplane captain."

Like we didn't know that.

The pilot was one of the nicer ones who never laughed at me or treated me like a dumb girl when I asked him questions about flying. He exited the airplane and walked down the steps. From the tarmac, he looked back up at the opening where the unknown woman stood. After she followed him down, he extended his elbow, and they stood side-by-side.

"Oh, my," the Braniff agent said. "Is that her beau?"

The stewardess was the next to leave the plane, followed by the other pilot. Then the foursome lined up, arm-in-arm, like they were ready to head down the aisle in a double wedding.

That's when the two men in the cabbie area made their move.

"What are they doing?" Calvin asked as the two men ran to the DC-3.

The man with the sign dropped it and blocked the quartet. He swung out his left arm to open his suit jacket, and the woman and the captain lifted their hands.

"Uh, oh," Rosie said.

The man gestured at the first officer and stewardess, and they raised their arms, too.

The second flashy man turned to the terminal window, pulled out a gun, and pointed it at us.

Myrna wasn't the only one in the crowd who gasped.

"Holy Moley, them two got guns!" Calvin shouted.

As if we hadn't noticed.

"I'm calling the police," the airport manager said as he bolted from the waiting area.

I figured it would be his second call. His first was probably to Amon Carter, the owner of the Fort Worth Star-Telegram, and the most powerful man in our part of the state. Everyone knew Carter liked to be the first to know things.

Outside by the airplane, Sign-Man pointed his gun at the woman that we assumed was Sally, grabbed her arm, and jerked her away from the captain. Second Flashy-Man stepped in front of the stunned pilot and gestured to the airplane. The two men climbed up the stairs and went inside.

"That guy is on *my* airplane," Rosie roared and rushed for the tarmac door.

Calvin and a Braniff mechanic were faster. They tackled Rosie and pinned him to the floor.

"You may be big, Rosie, but goons with guns win every time," the mechanic said. "If we rush in without a plan, someone will get hurt."

The men in the room nodded and retreated to a far corner to talk strategy while the women huddled on the opposite side. Myrna stayed by the window and watched the plane. It wasn't long before she called out, "That awful man is back."

Heads swiveled to the window. Second Flashy-Man stood in the airplane doorway. He pointed his gun at the stewardess, and she climbed up the stairs and went inside.

Myrna put her hands on her hips and looked back at Rosie. "Well, are you surprised that a stripper is associated with criminals?"

Rosie glared at her but kept his mouth shut.

I studied Sign-Man, who was guarding the woman and the second pilot. Something about those two guys didn't sit right with me, and it wasn't just their tacky clothes. Mr. Degas, my geometry teacher, said we should use logic when we worked through a problem. It didn't take me long to go through the knowns and unknowns about the men and wonder how they'd arrived at Meacham, since there wasn't a car parked in the taxi area.

With Myrna's attention on the airplane, the men arguing about tactics, and the women chattering about gun-toting criminals, no one saw me leave the waiting room. I went through the hangar and exited the big bay doors to the front of the airport. Sure enough, parked in the circular drive was a fancy black car. One that I'd only read about.

I returned to the waiting area where everyone was crowded around the window, watching the copilot walk up the airplane stairs. He disappeared inside, followed by Second Flashy-Man.

Once everyone stopped asking the same questions that no one could answer, I asked a new one. "Who owns the '33 Chrysler Imperial Phaeton parked out front?"

The airmail manager whistled. "A Phaeton? Didn't know we had any Rockefellers working here."

Even after I mentioned the car had a Louisiana license plate, no one claimed it. "Well, the owner is in for a surprise." I opened my fist and revealed a spark plug.

Myrna gasped like I'd helped myself to the money in the church collection plate. "Lillian, what have you done?"

"With only one plug, the car won't go as fast."

"That's exactly right, Miss Lily," Rosie said. He took the plug from me and slipped it into his pocket.

I hated it when people were surprised that I knew things.

"Really, Lillian," Myrna said. "Stealing parts from a car."

Rosie took a step forward and pointed his finger at her. "Those men pulled guns on the aircrew and us. When they are captured, Lily should get a reward."

I felt my face flush at Rosie's praise and bit my tongue to keep from sticking it out at Myrna. Instead, I turned to Gus, the owner, pilot, and mechanic of a one-man flying company. Before the rain stopped, he had a successful crop-dusting business. Now he was skipping meals and sleeping in his airplane. "You could help, too."

He cocked his head, and a patch of gray whiskers on his chin sparkled in the sunlight that streamed through the window next to him.

"Whatcha got in mind?"

"If those guys leave before the police get here, you could follow them." I raised an index finger and pointed up. "And report over the radio where they go."

Gus didn't answer, so I figured he didn't have enough money to buy a full tank of fuel. I pulled out my operating capital. His eyes widened at the dollar I held out. "Kid, I can't take your money," he said." You need—"

Rosie held up two bills and Calvin offered one.

Myrna squeezed past us, opened her pocketbook, and pulled out three more dollars. "Think of this as Christian charity. If you save that woman's life, maybe I can save her soul."

Gus stared at Myrna as if she'd offered to buy him a beer.

Although I'd never met Mr. Carter, I was sure that he'd pay us back and explained my logic. "Sally Rand is the star of his show. Once she's rescued, everyone will want to see her performance and he'll make even more money."

Myrna scowled.

"If she gets out of this alive," Gus said.

The Braniff ticket agent coughed. "Speaking of getting out. What if those men come in here and take us prisoner?"

If only she'd said that sooner.

The door to the waiting area opened with a bang. Second Flashy-Man walked in with his gun pointed at us. "Everyone, against the wall." He looked at Rosie, the biggest man in the room, and said, "You try anything, everyone gets it."

The door opened again and Sign-Man dragged in the woman we assumed was Sally. With one arm wrapped around her neck and a gun in his other hand, he watched us line up.

Myrna moved next to me and said, "Stay strong, girl. We will not be defeated by evil."

Second Flashy-Man's head whipped around, and he waved his gun at her. "Shut up or the kid gets it."

Myrna shut up.

With his free hand, he pointed to me and then flicked his finger to his side. "Come here. Now."

Myrna stepped forward. "Take me. She's just a child."

"If she ain't standing next to me in five seconds, you both are goners," he said.

As soon as I stepped forward, Second Flashy-Man grabbed me and stuck his gun in my ribs. "The kid'll be safe as long as nobody moves." He hustled me through the hangar door and out front to the black car. Sign-Man followed, dragging the woman from the airplane.

The men tied our hands behind us, and then Second Flashy-Man covered my eyes with a white handkerchief. I assumed the woman got the same treatment. Like a sack of potatoes, they tossed me into the back seat. Seconds later, something landed next to me.

"If one of you says anything, the other one gets it," a voice said, which I knew by then was Sign-Man. The car started and slowly pulled away, but it wasn't long before the men began to growl at each other like two angry hounds.

"What's wrong?" Sign-Man asked. "You forget how to drive?"

"It's the car. Something ain't right with it."

"It was fine earlier."

"Well, it ain't now."

Then the car turned, and Sign-Man erupted. "Whatta ya doing? Turn west, you dope. Drive toward the sun."

Second Flashy-Man hit the brakes. He shouted and cursed the car, fighting it like it was a wild horse.

The more the men argued, the more their accents and odd phrasing reminded me of someone, but I couldn't remember who. It wasn't anyone at school or Meacham. That left my neighbors. Not Sanchez, not Zywiki, not O'Halloran. Svenson, nope. Marchello. That was it. The men sounded like my neighbor, Babette Marchello, who was from New Orleans.

Once Second Flashy-Man had us going in the right direction, Sign-Man calmed down and went to bragging. "When the boss hears about this, he'll have me running this town."

"What do ya mean?" Second Flashy-Man asked. "This snatch ain't his idea?"

"Don't worry. I gotta plan. A local guy will take the fall. With him in jail, the boss takes over and—"

"Hey," Second Flashy-Man shouted. "There it is. Past the Kit Kat Klub sign."

When I heard that, I jerked in surprise and kicked the woman next to me, which caused her to utter a loud oof.

"Shut up," Sign-Man said.

Everyone at school knew that Danny Ahern's father owned the Kit Kat on Jacksboro Highway. During Prohibition, the not-so-secret speakeasy and gambling parlor was the center of North Texas bootlegging. Once alcohol was legal again, the Kit Kat became a legitimate supper club, although Ahern continued to run illegal booze out to the still-dry West Texas counties.

The car lurched left and bumped over a rough surface that rattled my teeth. After a sudden stop, hands yanked me out, dragged me over a gravel surface, and up three stairs. Nearby, unoiled hinges screeched in protest when someone opened a door. After another round of dragging, a push from behind sent me flying, and I landed on a wood floor.

Behind me, Sign-Man said, "Get the other one in here and don't take all day."

I heard a grunt and sensed a whoosh in the room. A door slammed and a lock clicked. I gave it ten seconds and then asked softly, "Is there someone here? My name is Lillian. Lily."

"I'm Sally," a voice whispered.

I waved my legs in different directions, trying to make contact with something, a wall, a door, or my fellow prisoner, but there was only empty air. "Sally, stretch out your legs. Can you touch anything?" Finally, something brushed my foot. "Do that again."

The second time, there was a tap on the bottom of my right shoe. Sally and I must have been in a straight line, feet-to-feet. Mr. Degas' geometry lecture on lines and angles came rushing back. I inch-wormed to the left, rolled on my right, then inch-wormed again to turn us into two parallel lines.

That's when Sally's patience gave out. "What are you doing? I can hear you moving."

"Trying to get close to you so that you can get to the butter knife in my pocket."

Once I was in the right place, she pawed at my dress and occasionally touched my leg and stomach. If a boy at school had done that, I'd have kicked him in the cojones. Since I'd never been kidnapped, tied up, blindfolded, and held captive, I made allowances.

After another round of grabbing, Sally said, "Got it. Now, turn away from me and wiggle your fingers so I can find the rope."

I made several more zigzags and shifted my arms until I felt a tug at my wrists.

"Twist and pull your hands apart," she said. "Is the rope any looser?"

It was, and I wiggled it off. After I freed Sally, she removed her blindfold and looked me over. Even though she'd seen me at Meacham, she still had to say it. "They sure grow 'em tall in Fort Worth."

A radio comedian, she wasn't.

With that old joke out of the way, I explored the room, which didn't take long. There was only the locked door, a corner ceiling hatch, and a window painted shut. I didn't know how to pick a lock, but the window I could handle. Every rent house I'd lived in had a few like that.

We took it slowly. I hacked at the window paint with my dull knife while Sally gently pushed on the sash. A screech from the warped wood would have brought our kidnappers barreling through the door faster than the law gunned down Bonnie and Clyde. Finally, we had the window open enough to slither through. Before I climbed out, I blew the paint flecks off the sill and scuffed up the floor dust. Once outside, I closed the window.

"Why did you do that?" Sally asked.

"To keep those guys guessing. If they think we're in the attic, it might give us more time to get away."

Now that we'd escaped from the kidnappers, we needed to hide and work out how to get back to Meacham. At the rear of the property was an out-of-control blackberry bush, and further back was a dark, dense mess of trees. I grabbed Sally's arm and pulled. "Come on, back there."

"Stop," she hissed. She waved an arm in the opposite direction. "I hear cars. We should go that way."

I was half her age, eight inches taller, and twice as strong. Sally Rand wasn't getting her way if I could help it. I tightened my grip and dragged her behind the blackberry bush, then bent close to her ear. "If there are windows on the front of the building, those guys will shoot us before we can wave down a car." She grew still, and I thought she agreed with my superior logic until I saw her staring up at an airplane making lazy figure eights in the distance.

It had to be Gus.

I yanked off my underskirt and moved to the far end of the blackberry bush so he could see me. I flapped the white cotton material up and down a few times, but it was as impressive as a bottle of hot Dr. Pepper. Sally ran into the trees behind us and returned with a branch that a storm had taken down.

"Use this."

I tied my petticoat flag to it and waved.

She watched the sky and, after a minute, said, "There, he saw you. He waggled his wings."

I missed the signal because I was watching a Mrs. Baird's Bread delivery truck pull behind the building in the next lot. "Sally, that's our escape."

Instead of congratulating me on the idea, she wrenched the tree branch from my hands, dropped to her knees, and pinched my thigh. "Get down and be quiet."

Through the blackberry brambles, we watched Sign-Man heave open the window that we'd crawled through. It protested with a loud shriek that Sally and I'd avoided. He stuck his head out, looked right, then left before shouting over his shoulder, "You idiot. They escaped."

Sally stuck out a shaky finger and whispered, "We have to leave."

I leaned in. "It's okay. He hasn't seen us."

"Not him," she said. "That."

I didn't know what she saw, but figured it was a snake. They loved to hide under blackberry bushes. They had all the berries they wanted, along with other animals that stopped by for a bite to eat.

Sign-Man disappeared from the window opening, and it was time Sally and I left, too. "Stand up slowly, back away, and run into the woods."

When no one came after us, we dodged from tree to tree until we were behind the store where the delivery truck was parked. We were about to run to it when a screen door squeaked a warning.

I stopped breathing.

The delivery man carried an empty wood carton to the back of his truck, exchanged it for a full one, and returned to the store. The second the store door slammed behind him, Sally and I hightailed it for the parking lot.

Canvas draped over arched metal ribs protected the cargo section of the truck and a separate curtain covered the back opening. I raised a corner of the material and peeked into the space. Along the right side of the truck bed was a row of empty cartons. I hoped that meant the driver was on his last delivery and would be leaving Jacksboro Highway.

Soon.

Sally and I climbed over the tailgate and were belly-down when the screen door screeched another warning.

I held my breath.

Light flashed to our right, and the floor vibrated as something slid across it. Seconds later, we were back in darkness.

The truck tilted to the left as the driver climbed into the cab. Then he began to crank the engine, which responded with a series of raspy wheezes.

I crossed my fingers.

Again and again, the driver tried to start the truck. Then silence. After thirty seconds, he made another attempt, and the motor responded with a rough rumble.

Sally sighed loudly.

Then came the driver's search for a working gear. After multiple rounds of metal-on-metal grinding, the truck jerked forward, then backward, sending Sally and me crashing into the empty cartons on the other side. After another change in direction, we ended up where we'd started. The truck jolted over rocks, then turned right onto a smoother surface.

I crawled to the tailgate and parted the curtain.

Big mistake.

The black Chrysler was riding our bumper. Sign-Man, in the passenger seat, raised his gun. I dove for the floor, yelling to Sally, "Stay down. Those guys are following us."

Seconds later, bullet holes riddled the canvas where I'd been standing. Behind us, the Chrysler's engine bellowed like an angry bull fixin' to charge.

"We're fish in a barrel," Sally said.

The delivery driver hit the gas pedal, which sent us sliding again. Then, as fast as the shooting started, it stopped.

"Reloading?" Sally asked.

I didn't know enough to answer. We crawled to the tailgate and crouched on opposite sides, where it would be less obvious for us to raise the curtain from the bottom.

She looked first and let out a gasp. "The plane we saw earlier is following those men."

I peeked and saw Sign-Man crawl out of the Chrysler's window, perch on the passenger door, and aim his gun up. "If he hits the plane, Gus is done for."

"Your friend is too high and too far back to be in danger," Sally said. "He's a good pilot. Maintaining his speed at that altitude isn't easy." She must have seen the doubt on my face. "I know. I'm a pilot, too."

I pushed her comment aside and focused on staying alive. "We need to do something while Gus has those guys distracted." I shifted three empty bread cartons closer to the tailgate and asked Sally, "What's going on out there?"

"The guy is still shooting at the airplane."

Exactly the answer I wanted. I balanced the first box on the tailgate, lifted the curtain, and shoved. Then I did it two more times.

With each launch, Sally whooped and cheered.

I made it back to my spot on the side of the truck in time to see the last carton bounce off the Chrysler's hood, hit the grill of an oncoming Ford truck, and ricochet back to hit the windshield in front of Second Flashy-Man. He jerked the steering wheel, causing the car to veer into the oncoming lane. It clipped a passing Buick, flew over a bar ditch, and went through a fence, which sent a herd of white-faced Herefords stampeding out of the way.

Sally grinned. "Nice work, kid. Now, what?"

As if the delivery driver had heard her question, the truck slowed to a stop. We lifted the curtain and looked into the smiling faces of two men wearing snow-white shirts and dark suits. The older man had a sweep of silver hair, and the younger one looked like Clark Gable. They were exactly what I imagined G-men looked like.

"Ladies, let us help you down," the older one said. "We'll take you back to your friends at Meacham while the police deal with the men who kidnapped you."

Their official-looking black four-door Chevrolet must have had all its spark plugs because the ride was speedy and smooth. When the airport came into view, I relaxed.

Big mistake.

The driver looked up into his cop-spotter mirror and said, "Boss, we gotta tail."

A shot rang out.

"Duck, ladies," the older man said. He leaned out of the passenger window, pointed his gun behind us, and fired. Seconds later, he roared with laughter. "Not quite a posse riding to the rescue. One shot and that pair turned tail and ran."

I raised my head above the back seat and snuck a look out of the window. A truck behind us turned down the side street that led to Meacham's rear entrance. Painted on its door was the name of the airline that Rosie and Calvin worked for.

My friends shot at us?

I turned forward and looked into the eyes of the driver, who was watching me in his mirror. Then he winked.

His gesture was a gut punch. The pieces of the mental jigsaw puzzle that I'd constructed to explain what was going on collapsed in a heap. G-men didn't rescue us. Fort Worth's most notorious bootlegger did.

Sally and I needed to escape.

Again.

I tapped her wrist twice and pointed to her door. She must have understood because she burst out of the car as fast as I did. Inside the terminal, Rosie and Calvin were waiting.

With weapons pointed *at us*.

"Hide in the hanger," Rosie said.

Sally and I only followed part of his command. We crouched on the other side of the door to the waiting room and cracked it open to hear what happened next.

"Paddy, be a man and show yourself," Rosie shouted.

When our rescuers walked into the waiting area with their hands held high, a new picture formed in my brain.

"You got it all wrong," the silver-haired man said. "We brought Sally Rand and the kid back. Didn't touch a hair on 'em."

Rosie and Calvin didn't lower their weapons.

I stood and motioned for Sally to follow me into the terminal. "He's right. The two men who took us are from New Orleans. They talked just like my neighbor. Remember, Rosie, I said the black Phaeton I took the spark plug from had a Louisiana license plate."

"The kid's right," the older man said. "The kidnappers are Carlos Santoro's boys."

Sally stepped forward. "Only Santoro didn't order the kidnapping. We overheard one of the men who took us say he wants a Fort Worth man to get blamed." She looked at the man with the fine head of hair. "Is that you? Are you the local man?"

He doffed his hat. "Paddy Ahern at your service, Miss Rand. Honored to meet you."

She gave him a star-studded smile.

Rosie harrumphed. He and Calvin lowered their weapons as Gus ran in from the tarmac.

"Ease up," Rosie called out. "Lily and Miss Rand are safe."

Gus crossed his arms and said to Paddy and his good-looking driver, "If you weren't working with those guys in the Chrysler, then how'd you know Lily and Sally Rand were in the bread truck?"

"I heard you talking to the Meacham tower when you were in the air," Paddy said.

"Those radio transmitters are restricted government equipment," Calvin said. "How'd you get one?"

Paddy flicked his wrist as if the question was silly. "I know people."

His answer left Gus, Rosie, and Calvin speechless.

I took advantage of their stunned silence and asked, "Sally, did you know you were going to be kidnapped? The airplane captain is usually the last to get off, but earlier, he left first."

She smiled. "Very observant, Lily. When I didn't see Mr. Carter's driver, I was suspicious of those men and alerted the crew."

"Your instinct was right," Rosie said. "Myrna checked with Carter's office. They canceled your pick-up after someone called and said you'd left the plane in St. Louis because you were sick."

"Why did the men take Lily?" Calvin asked.

"Insurance," Paddy said. "Since the Lindbergh kidnapping, snatching a kid gets everyone's attention."

Sally laughed. "Well, those men got it wrong. Lily isn't a helpless child. She gave as good as she got."

"No surprise, there," Rosie said.

I felt my face burn and rushed to change the subject. "What happened to the DC-3 crew?"

"Rosie and Calvin found them tied to the airplane seats and released them," Gus said.

While we waited for the police to arrive and take our statements, Sally made the rounds and thanked everyone for rescuing us. When she got to Gus, she complimented him on his flying and suggested that he give lessons.

Two days later, I was making pimento cheese sandwiches when Sally showed back up at Meacham with Mr. Carter's car and driver. She treated me to lunch downtown, then took me to the big bank where she helped me open a savings account and put in enough money to pay for flying lessons, two new dresses, and a new underskirt. I hoped that would keep Myrna off my back for a while, but I wasn't holding my breath.

—THE END—

About the Author

C.C. Guthrie writes mystery and crime short stories. She is a Derringer finalist, a finalist for the Bill Crider Prize for Short Fiction, and is a member of the SinC Guppy Chapter of Sisters in Crime as well as the Short Mystery Fiction Society.

The Snow Train

By Lise McClendon

DORIE LENNOX HUDDLED ON the platform in the frigid Missouri wind, waiting for the late train to Kansas City. St. Louis was her hometown's bookend, the other city on the river, slightly older and dirtier, well-worn with cattle, corn, soldiers, and ragtime. And now, three days before Christmas, families trying to keep smiling for their children, trying to get back to the farm, to the home place, to the relatives, through the heavy snow that blanketed the plains.

The big Christmas tree in the train station had shocked Dorie. She'd nearly forgotten about the holiday. She can't have been alone in this, not with the events of the month. It was two weeks since the devastation at Pearl Harbor. The reports were still coming in, every headline bringing fresh grief. Five battleships, sunk and gone. Many more ships grounded, beached.

Planes strafed on the ground. Thousands dead. The stories broke your heart, once, then again.

It took a full week of bad news for most people to rally, to change their thinking from avoiding the war to the reality of war. Japan, of course. They asked for it. When Germany and Italy declared war, we had no choice. We were in it up to our epaulets now. Dorie had barely slept that week, her emotions bouncing from hope to fear to hope again. Then hope was gone and action was all that remained.

She hadn't decided what she'd do yet, but she would be part of it somehow. A numbness had set in, disaster at every turn. She looked down the platform at the uniforms, soldiers embracing their wives, crying girlfriends and mothers, children clinging to pant legs, the handkerchiefs damp. It was already becoming too familiar. A man was looking back at her, not in uniform but in a long dark overcoat and brown hat on the back of his head, a lock of black hair flopped over his forehead. He was staring. She turned away, heart pounding.

The train approached, the sound of brakes squealing on the rails filling the frigid air. Dorie walked down the platform, away from the crowd. She stepped into the car as it stopped, throwing her small valise into the rack, sitting in an aisle seat to block an uninvited seatmate. Pulling her hat low over her eyes she leaned back, folding her arms, and feigned sleep. Passengers arrived in her car, shuffling, bumping, talking, sitting. She ignored them, snug in her rejection.

Someone bumped her knee. "Is that seat taken?" She stayed silent, hoping they would move on. She opened an eye, saw a black wool hem, scuffed oxfords. Closed her eyes again. "Excuse me." A briefcase was tossed across her onto the window seat. Dorie gritted her teeth. He could step over her legs. And he did, quickly, onto the seat.

She sighed and pushed her brim back. Harvey Talbot looked quite pleased with himself.

"Miss Doria Lennox. As I live and breathe." He grinned like a monkey then cocked an eyebrow. "Too much? I've been in Alabama."

Dorie rearranged herself, pulling in her feet and sitting tall. What should she say to him? She couldn't think of a thing. Luckily, he kept talking.

"Fancy running into you. What brings you to old St. Louie? Or have you been traveling?" She shrugged, hoping he'd just stop now. He set his briefcase by his feet and turned in his seat. "I can wait all night. With this snowstorm it might take that long to get home."

Their affair, or whatever you called it, had only lasted a few months. That was two years ago and it was over. But he still had the ability to make her heart race and it was annoying. Best to act normal and wait for it to pass.

"What were you doing in Alabama?" she asked smoothly.

"Checking on the progress of the pilots down at Tuskegee."

"How's that going?" Dorie had a stab of envy for those pilots, for their adventure, dangerous as it would be. Someday she would fly a plane. She'd made a promise to herself.

"Good. Quite a story, if I do say so myself. The Ninety-Ninth Pursuit Squadron they're calling them. They're still talking about Mrs. Roosevelt down there. I interviewed the pilot who took her up."

She nodded, tugging on her hat.

"Your turn," he said. "What've you been up to?"

She swallowed hard. "Seeing somebody off. I rode over with him." She glanced at Harvey, checking how that information was taken.

His eyes hardened. "I'm sorry. There's a lot of that these days."

She put her hands under her legs. Wasn't he curious who she'd seen off? Maybe he was over her. The ring on her left hand tapped on the wooden seat. It felt odd. She'd meant to take it off.

He'd noticed it. "When did you get married?"

"Last week," she said quickly, as if that was all there was to it. "After he enlisted. What about—?" She bit off her words. Too personal.

"What about me? Why haven't I enlisted?" He folded his arms and lowered his eyebrows angrily. "Are you questioning my patriotism?"

"No. No, I'm sorry. I didn't mean that." His glower eased. "Where were you on December 7th?"

"Working the weekend shift. We got the news on the teletype."

"Terrible day."

"Terrible week."

He gave a short nod. "Where were you?"

"Nowhere. At the boarding house. We listened to the radio all day. And bought the *Star*, of course." She gave him a little conciliatory smile. It wasn't so bad, nice really, having him here on the long ride home. Someone who knew her, someone to talk to. The train had pulled out of the station, moving slowly past the stockyards, the shanties, the pastures and fields, out to the river. "It's been a while, hasn't it? Since we've talked."

He glanced at her, then turned to the window, silent. The snow along the tracks was thick and piled under the nearby street lamps like giant whipped cream sodas with a straw. The click-clack of the wheels was slow, methodical, promising a long night.

"My mother asked about you, at the end."

Dorie startled. "At the—? Is she—?"

"In November. I thought you might have seen the notice in the *Star*."

Impulsively she took his large hand. It was cold. "I'm so sorry. If I'd known I would have come."

He was staring at her hand around his. He tightened his grip and looked out at the night. It was dark and silent outside the city. Even the mighty Missouri was cloaked, invisible. Snow fell sideways across the glass. They sat like that until the ticket agent came by and the spell was broken.

Settling again, she asked, "Did she suffer? I hope not."

"Not much. It was her heart. It gave out." He looked at her, composed again. "How is Amos?"

Her boss in the detective agency, Amos Haddam, was a scraggly old Brit. His health was compromised during the war, the first one, by mustard gas. "Still ticking. Looks like hell, though."

"That's nothing new." Amos liked Harvey and often asked about him, like Harvey's mother apparently did about her. She thought about Joe then, guiltily, as if she'd forgotten what had happened over the last two weeks. Her *husband*. How odd, that word. She concentrated on his face, his blond hair and bullish neck, and what it made her feel, or didn't. She crossed her fingers in her lap. He would come home, whatever she felt about him. She would answer every letter, no matter what.

"This snow is something, isn't it?" she said. There was nothing to see now, just blackness and their reflected faces on the windowpane. Harvey nodded at her, their eyes meeting. Why had she broken up with him? Or did he end things? She couldn't really remember. Harvey was her first stand-up boyfriend, the sort of man who fought for people, for the right things, for truth. The kind of man she never thought she deserved, a strong, brave man, a good man. She remembered how he had discovered their neighborhood stiff was a ragtime piano player and how Harvey got him banging the ivories out in the street. Now that was a day.

It was fifteen minutes of silence before he got up the nerve to ask. "So, who's the lucky fella?"

"We met on a case. The girl who died on the tracks in October. Do you remember that one?"

"Sort of. She got her leg cut off?"

"There was freezing rain that night, and it was slippery. She was walking along the tracks, that was the guess. She fell, or something, and the train ran over her leg. She bled to death."

"How old?"

"Sixteen. Her name was Blanche Forsythe. She was his sister. Joe, that's his name."

"Joe Forsythe. Nope, I don't know him."

"You wouldn't. He works — worked — at the stockyards." Joe's odor was his legacy, she thought. If she never saw Joe again, if he never came back from the war, she'd always remember his smell. "Blanche, believe it or not, worked in a laundry as a bleacher."

"Blanche the bleacher? Sounds like a chorus girl." He smiled then winced. "Sorry. Rest in peace, Blanche."

"She walked to work along the tracks most days, even though she wasn't supposed to. It was the fastest way from their house to the laundry. But it was a Sunday morning when it happened. So, the cops figured she was walking to church."

"Let me guess. The church was in the other direction."

"Righty-o, as Amos would say. But the cops didn't care. By the time they found her, there was no evidence left. The freezing rain had turned to regular rain, washing down the scene."

"So, Joe asked you to look into it? And what did you find, madam shamus?"

"Not much at first. Lots of legwork, not many answers."

"But you didn't give up. Not you. Let me guess how it went. You looked for a boyfriend first."

"Well, after I talked to everyone at the laundry, at home, and at church, yes. She had been in school until the year before and there was a boyfriend from school. He didn't know anything, hadn't seen her for months."

"Scratch boyfriend number one. On to number two."

"How'd you know? Seems nights when her folks thought she was at some knitting circle she was over on the wrong side of town."

"She had a boyfriend of a different color?" Harvey raised his eyebrows dramatically. "How modern."

"Not everybody thought it was a good idea. In fact, nobody did. The boyfriend is a sort of man-about-town. You might know him." She paused. "Winslow Jones."

"The actor?"

"And theater owner, and club impresario. Winslow has fingers in a lot of pies."

"And his arms around a lot of women, I hear."

"He's a handsome man." Winslow Jones was more than handsome, she thought to herself. He was the sort of brown-skinned gigolo mothers worry about and daughters dream about. Six-foot-two with a pencil-mustache and made hair, a broad chest, yellow eyes, and dancing hips. Winslow had no shortage of admirers.

"Who knew about the two of them? Her parents?"

"They're good Christian folk. She had them fooled. But Blanche got herself dolled up and swanned over to his clip joint a couple times. Where some of Winslow's other women got a good gander."

"Isn't he married?"

"The wife was one of the dames at the club. Caused a good old catfight, they say."

"The wife pushed her under the train?"

"Not so fast, slick." Dorie nudged him. "Winslow runs some hotcha girls out of the club. You know the type."

He grinned. "I have no idea what you mean."

"Uh-huh. There's one you might have heard of. A real fancy girl, Lola Champagne. That's her stage name."

"Lola Champagne? Doesn't ring a bell."

"She's a fan dancer, you know, big feathers, coupla baubles, and not much else." He was grinning again. "You're familiar with her work. I don't get to burlesque joints very often."

"Me neither. Feathers make me nostalgic. Or allergic."

"Lola was supposed to work that night. She did her dance act and then she met her customer at his table. I could tell you the name of her customer, he was pretty open with me. But he's in… government work." She whispered that last bit. "Confidential." She crossed her heart with a finger. Her lips were sealed. The assistant district attorney had threatened her with jail time on her old warrant if she blabbed.

"A public servant? How shocking."

The brakes of the train squealed loudly and they were thrown forward. Harvey put his arm across to brace Dorie. Her collar bone bumped his elbow. The train screeched and came to a stop. All around them in the car, passengers groaned, waking up and cross about it. A suitcase tipped off the rack and landed on a man's bald head. That caused a ten-minute ruckus. Harvey helped calm the duffer down, offering to go get ice from the club car for his bump. The man refused, taking his broken head down there himself.

By the time Harvey sat down again, Dorie had scooted into his window seat. "Want it back? There's nothing to see but acres of white."

He demurred, pulling his overcoat around him again and tightening his wool scarf. "It's freezing in here. Got gloves?" Dorie found her old brown leather gloves in her pockets and slipped them on. They were thin, useless as tits on a rooster. She plunged her hands into her coat pockets. At least she'd worn trousers. They could see their breath now, clouds of winter around their heads.

"You think there's snow on the track?"

"Or cattle. Or both."

They sat contemplating the situation, feeling colder by the minute. After a long pause when nothing seemed to be happening to get the train going, Harvey reached into his suit pocket and pulled out a flask. "A little hooch for what ails ya?"

Dorie unscrewed it and took a gulp, feeling the liquor burn then warm her feet and hands. "I feel better already." Harvey drank and slipped the flask back inside his coat.

"So, Miss Lola Champagne and Loyal Public Servant were deep in conversation at the Zoot Club," he said, prompting her to continue.

"Right, the Zoot Club." She squinted at him. "She makes nice then gets a phone call and never comes back."

"Where'd she go?"

"The coat check floozie says the phone call was from Blanche."

"They meet up? Why?"

"Wondered that myself. Nobody remembered they even knew each other. But Winslow Jones shed some light on that. He admitted, after some careful prodding and superior sleuthing, that Lola Champagne is really Gustine Jones."

"Winslow's sister?"

"Got it in one. Care to speculate?"

Harvey bit his lips, thinking. "Blanche is going to expose Lola's identity, embarrassing her brother?"

"Not much embarrasses a man like Winslow Jones."

"Embarrass Lola then. But she's totally exposed." He wiggled his eyebrows. " Or so I'm told." Dorie smiled. He said, "Blanche is blackmailing somebody."

"Getting warm."

He rubbed his hands together. "I wish. The wife already knows about Blanche. Okay, gumshoe. Who is Blanche blackmailing?"

A steward stepped into the car, carrying a pile of gray blankets. A murmur of relief went through the passengers as he handed them out. Harvey and Dorie wrapped theirs around their shoulders. Dorie pulled her feet up, tucking them in. Harvey asked the steward about the situation. "Going to be a while, sir. Big drift across the tracks."

After the steward left, they shared another sip from the flask. "Okay?" Harvey asked Dorie. She nodded, although her lips had begun to quiver. Outside, the wind buffeted the train cars, rocking them as the howl sang along the rails. "Damn. Hold on." He unwound his blanket and tugged hers loose. Then wrapped both blankets around them together, sliding closer, linking his arm through hers. "Strength in numbers, Lennox."

Dorie felt his body, close and comforting. Soon her lips stopped shaking. She took his hand under the blanket, squeezing it. "Warmth in numbers, Talbot." She looked at him, his hat pulled low. "Your ears are turning white." He pulled his plaid scarf over his head like a Russian woman and replaced his hat, turning up the collar of his coat.

"How's that?" he asked and she laughed. They sat, shivering, silent, wiggling toes and fingers. A child somewhere behind them began to cry. "Tell me the story, Lennox."

"Right. I was stumped after I found out Blanche was a squeeze of Winslow Jones, and that Lola Champagne is Winslow's sister. Then everybody clammed up."

"Did you have to cut 'em with your pig sticker?"

"I'm leaving my switchblade at home these days. Too much trouble. As you recollect."

"What's your sweetener then?"

"Squawking to coppers. Works sometimes with mugs like Jones. I counted fourteen laws he was breaking in five minutes in the Zoot Club."

"Sounds about right. Did he crow?"

"Nope. Got friends in high places, he says. But Lola? She's been busted dozens of times. No more jail-time, she said. Real shaky, she was, like somebody else was leaning on her, too. She's a looker in her clothes, in case you were wondering."

"In or out, I'd say. Who was leaning on her? Our public servant?"

"One of his friends." She squeezed his hand. "Maybe you should think about writing for a newspaper or something, wise guy? This other public servant is all straight-up proper. Methodist or something. Doesn't cotton to fancy girls. Lola told me that Blanche was blackmailing Winslow. She was going to tell the cops he was having relations across the race line if he didn't pay up. Gambling, prostitution, burlesque, hell, ballot stuffing: all good in Kansas City. But the race line?"

"Painted in blood." He glanced at her. "How'd he do it?"

"He and Lola got her drunk. Maybe slipped her a mickey. She was out cold. They dumped her on the tracks. There's an underpass near where she was found. Easy for the two of them to haul her down."

"So, strictly speaking, they didn't kill her?"

Dorie shook her head. "Their story is they dropped her off, drunk as a skunk. Never saw her again." She looked out the window. She hadn't seen Blanche's body. It had been swept off to an early burial. Just as well, but Dorie's mind's eye was vivid and disturbing.

"Lola told you all this?" Harvey asked.

"I saw her lift a purse in the club. I promised not to turn her in if she spilled. I told the cops the whole thing but Winslow pays them off to stay in business. They don't want that gravy train to dry up."

"Your word against theirs. That's bushwa." He put his other hand around her fingers. "At least you got the truth. Most don't care."

"It's a job."

"Big money, huh?" He gave her a sympathetic smile. "That's what I thought."

Around them the car quieted as people snuggled into the night and the thin gray railway blankets. The bare ceiling bulbs flickered and went out. Harvey pulled her closer. "Are you warm?" he whispered.

"Enough. With you." In the dark she leaned her head on his shoulder. He leaned his head on hers. It was pleasant. But she hoped the train got going soon, before they all turned into icicles. She closed her eyes and felt the tug of sleep.

After a minute, Harvey blurted out: "What's he like? Your Joe."

She blinked her eyes and straightened up. "Ah, you know. Just a fella." Nothing special, she wanted to say, because Joe was just a Joe. "Kind of a shit-kicker."

"Farmer?"

"Feeds cattle down at the yards. Smells like it."

Harvey laughed. "Sounds like a catch." His voice lowered again. "Do you love him?"

Dorie looked at him through the gloom, his face now shaded with a dark beard. He'd pulled down the scarf and caught her eye, making her confess. She felt so close to him suddenly, as if there was no one else in the world she could talk to. Maybe there wasn't.

"I felt sorry for Joe," she admitted. "His sister died, horribly. He was wrecked. The parents were wrecked. Then Pearl Harbor hit us all and he ran right out and enlisted like a bunny. Not that everybody who enlisted is a bunny... but Joe? He didn't think about it. He was crying and shouting and running crazy."

"One of the copy boys did the same thing."

"Then he sorta came to his senses. Said he couldn't sleep, kept having nightmares of getting blown to smithereens and his parents having no kids to take care of them in their old age. He's all they've got now. He shoulda thought about that."

Harvey was massaging one her hands. But he didn't ask for details. He just waited until she was ready. Such a patient man. You'd have to be patient to get involved with Dorie Lennox, she thought. She took a deep breath and blessed the dark.

"So, he says, begs really: let's get married. It'll keep me alive, he says. Write me every day, he says. You can take care of my old mother since yours is gone. I didn't want to. I barely knew him and truth be told he's about as big as a button and not as cute, with hair like straw and pink cheeks and tons of freckles. And as hard as he washes, he can't get that stink off him. He says nobody notices but me, but they're lying. They are definitely pulling a windy on that one." Harvey chuckled. "But he won't leave me alone. There's no work really, not since December 7th. I can't get rid of him that way. So finally, we get really drunk like everybody else on the day we go to war with Germany and we do it. We get the license. We were too squiffy to actually stand up and say, 'I do.'"

"You got rings?"

"He gave me one. Probably out of a Cracker Jack box."

"And you're happy?"

Happy? Her throat closed and she thought she might cry. "Oh, Harvey," she croaked. She was so far from happy. The thing with Joe was all wet. Harvey moved under the blanket, his long arms circling her shoulders. With her face against his coat, she babbled out her misery. "I didn't turn it in, the license. I looked at it and I just couldn't. He left it with me. Does that mean...?"

He didn't answer. It was her question, her answer. She had to decide whether the marriage was real or not.

"I didn't want to hurt him," she finally said.

After a moment he asked: "How was your wedding night?" Just like that, with a hard edge of jealousy in his voice. Maybe he felt he could ask because they were lovers once, they knew each other's scars and soft spots. She wasn't squeamish about sex like a lot of girls. She wasn't like a lot of girls. And she had nothing to hide from Harvey Talbot.

"We were blind drunk. Somebody down the street was passing around a bottle of moonshine. He tried, but... he passed out, then went back to his mother's house. She was expecting him."

"How old is your Joe?"

"Eighteen. I know. I've got close to ten years on him. He'll probably find some cute Frenchie and forget about me." She sighed. "I hope."

Harvey pulled back. "Do you hope?" He tucked a loose hair behind her ear.

She looked into his eyes, unreadable in the dark. He smelled so nice, like cinnamon and smokes, the way he always did. This was the last thing she thought would happen on the night train to Kansas City in the middle of the worst snowstorm in a decade. But she'd never been one to second-guess fate. Except perhaps in the case of Joe.

Did she hope? There, in a train stuck in the snow in the darkest of winter nights, with no stars to guide them home, in the bitter wind and cold, with war everywhere, with death and destruction and bombs and torpedoes, with all that, she felt something stir in her heart. Things wouldn't be this bad forever. She could hope again. Not because of Joe. That mistake would be undone somehow.

"Kiss me, Talbot," she whispered. "My lips are cold."

—THE END—

About the Author

Lise McClendon is the author of numerous novels and short stories, including the Bennett Sisters mysteries, Rory Tate thrillers, Dorie Lennox mysteries, and the Alix Thorssen mysteries. She also wrote and directed the short film, *The Hoodoo Artist*. Lise has served on the national boards of directors for Mystery Writers of America and International Association of Crime Writers/North America. She splits her time between Montana and Southern California. Learn more about Lise and her work at www.lisemcclendon.com.

Woe In the Windy City

By Joe Kilgore

Chicago 1943

SNOW CUPCAKED THE BANISTER of the rowhouse stoop. It was March, and the weather was contemptuous of anyone hoping for an early spring. At least a path had been cleared on the sidewalk, Porter ruminated. Either by the never-ending slog of the working class or the act of a good Samaritan. Porter's money was on the former. The latter was a sucker's bet. Good Samaritans in his neighborhood were scarce as Republicans. It wasn't that the denizens of North Avenue, bordered by Clark and Ogden, were antisocial — or maybe it was. Less than favorable news from the war often chilled camaraderie the same way winds off Lake Michigan chafed uncovered ears. But you could get past the distress of one and the sting of the other in

The Twin Anchors, a local pub that opened early, served food as well as drink, and, day or night, provided at least some degree of respite from relentless winter. Porter often found himself there at eight o'clock in the morning washing down scrambled eggs and sausage with a cold Pabst Blue Ribbon. He wasn't an alcoholic. Hot coffee would come later at work. The man simply had his priorities.

Work was a photography shop where he earned his wages providing maintenance and repairs for individuals with their Konicas and Leicas or businesses with a Burke & James or a Bell & Howell. Porter knew the ins and outs of most well-known brands. For his own personal use, however, he had chosen a Graflex Ciro 35. Small and unobtrusive, at 18 ounces it was easy to carry, and he appreciated the range finder focusing that provided great depth of field. Its 50 mm lens assured his pictures would virtually always be in sharp focus. That was important to Porter — clarity being an essential component of blackmail.

No one starts out to be an extortionist. Well, virtually no one. Most simply grow into it. A kid sees his big sister knock over their mother's favorite vase. She begs him to go along with her story that the cat did it. He complies in return for that Hershey Bar she was saving. Years later he spots her being kissed and felt up by that lameo with the letter jacket. The sibling's compensation for keeping mum has increased to the price of a movie ticket plus soda and popcorn. Of course, while the ill-gotten gains are nice, the real payoff is the control he can exert over someone who thinks she can boss him around just because she's older and assumes she knows more. He knows real power is not just knowledge, but knowledge of bad behavior. It's coin of the realm if one is willing to threaten vulnerable individuals with the prospect of public shame. And for the right price, who isn't?

Porter never had a sister. His addiction to coercion grew out of an insatiable need for revenge. Reprisal for a childhood marred by supposedly standup members of the community. The small town he grew up in was even thinner in tolerance than it was in nonconformity. That's why Porter's unwed mother and he were the butt of gossip. So much so that his schoolmates, fueled by their loose-lipped parents' scandalmongering, took to calling him no-name, bastard-boy, and whore's-spawn. The kids may not have known what all of those monikers meant, but they could see the pain and embarrassment on Porter's face that the nicknames inflicted. So naturally, being the purveyors of cruelty that most children are, they harassed him mercilessly. Nearly to a point of no return. One wouldn't have thought it could go as far as it did, but that's only because one sometimes forgets the inherent dangers of asinine people in groups.

It was a gaggle of pre-pubescent dullards that took it upon themselves to do something about this abhorrent stain with which their parents seemed fixated. One chilly November afternoon they lay in wait for bastard-boy as he walked home from school. While young Porter was used to altering his route when he saw this or that bully approaching, the overwhelming number of collective miscreants quickly surrounded him and cut off avenues of escape. A pillowcase was thrown over his head. He was pushed and shoved. His arms were squeezed and pinched as he was made to stumble forward in darkness. Continual manhandling spiked his fear and rendered him incapable of keeping his bladder in check. The youngster pissed his pants as his doleful pleas for release were met with laughter and insults.

After being rushed along for some time and kept upright only by the vice grip of gloved fingers, the creak of an opening door and a change in temperature told the captive what his abductors wouldn't. They were no longer outside. They were somewhere infinitely quieter but only slightly less cold.

"Sit him there," he heard one of them say as they forced him down on the floor and yanked him backward until his spine banged into a wall. "Now, bastard-boy, count to a hundred," the same voice said, "and don't take that cover off your head until you reach ninety-nine. One of us is going to stay with you to see that you don't." More giggling. More insults. "Count slower, and louder no-name, we can't hear you." Young Porter's small voice grew bigger as one-by-one he began to rattle off numbers. The shanghaiers' laughter grew fainter and more distant until eventually all that Porter heard was his own voice saying "40, 41, 42..." By the time he got to 75, the silence surrounding his count was deafening. He paused and steeled himself for a punch from whomever had been left behind to harass him. Nothing. But he continued to count silently and when he reached 100, he slowly slid the pillowcase up, then off his head. He could have done the same at 60.

Alone now, he initially felt a moment of relief — joy even that he was no longer encircled by the hyenas that had waylaid him. But reality has a way of amputating contentment without anesthetic. Where was he? What was this place? How far was it from home?

While the tiny police force took the information Porter's frantic mother related about her missing son, their actual interest in it was something less than intense. Just another kid running off, they immediately assumed. Porter's mom knew better — realizing that while the child had plenty to run from, he had no place to run to.

It would be days before the boy found his way out of the interlocking work rooms and made his way through the intricate design network of the abandoned factory. During those days, he subsisted only on the jellybeans he had previously stuffed in his pocket for safe keeping, and the foul smelling brown liquid that often started, stopped, then violently spat itself from various pipes. Pipes that had rusted on the outside and coated themselves on the inside with various chemicals and debris from tiny creatures that slithered rather than scurried like the rats who shared young Porter's prison.

Eventually, summoning the perseverance to keep looking until he found a way out of the metal and mildewed maze, the boy was able to locate an exit with a door to the outside world. He had overcome his fear, steeled his resolve, and somehow survived. But not without cost. The foul water and diluted chemicals he had ingested in the factory would find their way into more than one of the youngster's vital organs, retarding their healthy development and stunting the growth of the child physically, plus leaving him with omnipresent dyspepsia that would lead to additional abnormalities as he grew.

Following the incident, local authorities dubbed it a childhood prank by a group of youthful adolescents and therefore unworthy of official punishment. So Porter and his mother soon left their intolerant hamlet for the welcoming anonymity of the Windy City. She brought with her an unrelenting commitment to raising her son, even if it took — and it did — the repellent process of trading her body for the necessary funds to do so. In addition to his physical ills, Porter brought with him a disorder contracted from both his long-suffering childhood and his short but unforgettable confinement. An ailment of the mind that, as he matured, would metastasize into an insatiable appetite to find the self-satisfied and contented and somehow work out a way to smear them with indelible shame.

ROGER GAMMON WAS A prime example of the kind of person Porter hated; tall, good-looking, well-dressed, successful. A relatively young man at thirty-four, Roger avoided service in the war due to an arrhythmic heart condition. Medication kept it in check and him stateside while others his age were fighting and dying in Europe and the South Pacific. Roger took advantage of this situation in multiple ways. He married, fathered two children, and served as an exceptional provider for his wife and family. He outworked his older male coworkers and rose rapidly through the ranks of the insurance agency that employed him. Simultaneously, Roger sport-fucked his way through the ever-expanding secretarial staff. Young lovelies, lonely for their husbands and boyfriends far away, were particularly susceptible to Roger's initial friendliness, which soon transitioned into innuendo-filled compliments, eventually leading to passion-filled assignations in stairwells, storerooms, and offices that could be locked from the inside. Only on rare occasions would Roger intertwine with his conquests in a hotel or where they lived. He was not fond of spending money for the former and concerned about accidentally being seen near the latter. Plus, there was a decidedly lurid quality about bumping uglies on top of indemnity forms and actuarial tables that increased the intensity of Roger's climaxes exponentially.

Roger crossed Porter's path when he decided to buy his wife a small camera which would enable her to document their two growing daughters' progress though life. Porter immediately found Roger's smug attitude distasteful. Along with the younger man's assumption that anyone would be remotely interested in the particulars of his conventional family. So, after the sale was completed, and making up an excuse about a necessary doctor's appointment, Porter sought and received permission to take his lunch an hour early. In truth, he simply wanted to follow the garrulous customer whom Porter deemed too self-satisfied by half. Through years of analyzing human nature, Porter had come to the conclusion that those who engage in overt displays of verbosity often have even more to hide than they do to share. Such was the case, he bet, with the pompous ass who walked out of his employer's store with a new Kodak Pony 828.

Adept at stalking, Porter had honed his reconnaissance techniques over time. Often he would simply pick out an individual on the street and trail them until they vanished into a row house or apartment building. Keeping his distance, he would employ moves to avoid suspicion should the unknowing subject turn around for one reason or another. Quickly gazing into a shop window, he would feign interest in whatever was on display. Were no such windows available, he would stoop to tie his already tied shoelace. Only on rare occasions would he actually turn and walk away from his prey, knowing the jig would be up if he were spotted a second time. He never was. Porter enjoyed the hunt.

Roger headed back to the skyscraper where he worked, not knowing that eyes were on him. Porter even followed him into the building and stayed close enough to hear him say "Fifteen, please," to the elevator operator. Once its doors closed and headed skyward, Porter went to the building directory in the lobby. He noted that the only business listed on the fifteenth floor was American Eagle Life Insurance. *I should have guessed. Who else could be that boring*, Porter said to himself.

After returning to his own place of business, Porter made a call to American Eagle Life Insurance. He asked about and received their hours of operation from a congenial female voice. Fate was apparently on his side. The insurance company closed their business day half an hour after the camera shop closed theirs. That would make it easy for Porter to take up a position outside the building where he could see everyone departing without anyone seeing him. There he would wait, and watch, for as long as it took. Then he would follow. Knowing where Roger lived, where he went after work, whether he went straight home, or whether he had any routine at all was vitally important. Porter already had the impetus to stalk his new prey. Now all he needed was the time to do it. He'd make time.

Hazel Balentine was Roger's latest conquest. A saucy redhead from Des Plaines, Hazel enjoyed sharing the sheets as much as anyone. While she knew there was no likelihood of a long-term relationship, she hoped there might be short-term gain in salary and status by shtupping her superior who couldn't keep his eyes off her exceptionally bell-shaped bottom. Refusing rushed office trysts, however, she let Roger know that the only way he was going to get in her knickers was to come through her front door — no pun intended. Roger relaxed his aversion to playing his game on her home turf because, simply put, the prize far outweighed the principle.

Hazel lived on the ground floor of a two-story duplex. Porter couldn't believe his luck when he found a window on the alley side of the house that afforded a front row seat to feats of acrobatic fornicating he never imagined possible. One picture after another documented the pair's couplings in graphic detail. But Porter didn't stop there. He had a feeling that his newfound lothario was probably not a one-off adulterer. His instinct proved correct when, one midday, he followed Roger and a female coworker ostensibly on their way to lunch. The noon time meal turned out to be cunnilingus on the trunk of a Packard in the corner of an indoor parking lot. In three weeks, Porter had enough snapshots to amass an album of indiscretion.

The first pictures arrived at American Eagle Life Insurance in a plain 8 1/2" X 11" envelope with Roger's full name and address on the outside, along with the words PERSONAL

& CONFIDENTIAL, TO BE OPENED BY ADDRESSEE ONLY. Roger's personal secretary — whom he hadn't gotten around to boffing just yet — abided by the stern directive and placed the envelope on her boss's desk along with the remainder of his morning mail. Roger arrived, began going through the stack, took note of the odd envelope, opened it, and involuntarily boomed, "Jesus Fucking Christ!"

"Mr. Gammon, are you all right? Can I help with something?" his secretary asked.

"Ah... no. I'm fine. Just stay at your desk. I'm okay. No problem"

There's something disconcerting about seeing one's private parts on full display for the world to ogle. Especially when those parts are involved in remarkably compromising positions. Roger had never seen his manliness in photographs before. The experience was not totally unpleasant. There was an initial moment of lurid fascination, however, that quickly gave way to embarrassment followed almost immediately by fear. A sickening realization overwhelmed him. Someone had taken these pictures and was planning to do something awful with them. Something that could ruin his job, his marriage, his family. Something that could turn Roger's storybook life into a hideous exposé of lust, lies, and shame. Where was it? The note. There must be a note. There must be. But there wasn't one. What the hell was going on?

DURING THE TIME THAT Porter had been compiling his pictorial dossier of Roger's various transgressions, he had occasion to see the insurance executive out with his wife and children. The girls were as cute and charming as youngsters in Marshall Field's Department Store ads. His wife, Grace, seemed the epitome of loveliness and decorum. That's when the idea started to form in his head. An idea he couldn't seem to shake. An idea that invaded his dreams at night. Why not? Why couldn't he? Why shouldn't he? Why was something like that beyond him? Especially after all he had been through. Didn't he deserve it? Didn't he deserve it just once?

Heretofore, Porter had always done a cash and carry business. He'd hook the mark with explicit photos. Name a price to be paid for the negative and prints. Arrange for a drop and pickup. Then move on to his next victim with money in his pocket and secure in the knowledge that another sanctimonious and hypocritical asshole had been fully and completely scared shitless. He particularly liked the fact that the poor sods never could be completely sure that he wouldn't return at some time in the future to make their life miserable again. Yes. It was a formula that had worked well for him. But this time, why not? Why not get something special to forever remember the Gammons.

———

GRACE GAMMON WAS EVERYTHING she appeared to be. Attractive, charming, a wonderful wife and devoted mother. She came from good Gold Coast stock. Her father was a banking executive and her mother a socialite of the first order. It was said Carl Sandburg used to read unpublished poems at their Sunday soirees. Yes, Grace's parents provided her with everything she needed to succeed in life, and Roger provided her with everything she wanted: a handsome, affectionate husband who could keep her and their children nestled nicely in the lifestyle to which she had long been accustomed. As such, it was easy for Grace to exude her namesake to virtually everyone with whom she came in contact. Retailers and tradespeople she addressed by name. Friends' and acquaintances' birthdays and anniversaries were always remembered with a call or a card. It literally never occurred to her that their family's idyllic lifestyle could be compromised in any way. But it occurred to Porter.

———

ROGER WAS ON PINS and needles for days. The explicit photos had rocked him. Was one of his conquests involved? Surely none pictured, he assumed. Why had no one taken responsibility? Why were there no demands? Were there more shocks to come? Would something show up, not just at his office, but also at his home? Roger lost sleep. His work suffered. He was late for meetings. He even lost his appetite for frequent dalliances. Then it came. Returning home, opening the door, and seeing the envelopes still on the floor that had been pushed through the mail slot, Roger immediately saw what he hoped he wouldn't see. This time in a regular letter-sized envelope, but with the same printed admonition: PERSONAL & CONFIDENTIAL. TO BE OPENED BY ADDRESSEE ONLY. Clutching it to his chest, he looked around to see if anyone was watching. Apparently not. Holding it up to the light, he could tell there were no photos inside. Just a folded piece of paper. Roger tore open one edge, slid the note out and read it:

I don't want money. I only want to do what you're doing with those women. Except, I want to do it with your wife. One time. Then you'll never hear from me again. Prints and negatives will be destroyed. If you don't comply, pictures will be sent to your employer, your associates, your clients, your friends, your family, your wife's family, your daughter's school. My next note will provide a place and time for your wife to arrive. Any attempt to bring in the authorities will trigger release of the photos. Have a nice day.

Roger was stunned. What kind of sick individual was this? How could anyone think he could possibly comply with such a request? And not just him. What about Grace? Obviously, there was no way she'd ever consent to such an atrocity. No wife would. There was no way he could ask her. But what was he to do? Nothing, he thought. At least for the moment. He'd do nothing and see if the next note came. Maybe fate would intervene. Maybe the vile blackmailer would get run over by a truck, fall on the tracks of the EL, or be done in by some other poor schmo whose life he was also trying to ruin. Maybe it would all go away... somehow.

When Roger arrived at work two days later, the next note was waiting for him:

Drake Hotel, Room 401, Saturday, 8 p.m. She must come alone. No tricks.

Fate had not lent a hand. It was now Thursday. At day's end, Roger's long night of the soul began as most of his evenings did. Upon his arrival at home, Grace fixed him a cocktail. They ate dinner with the girls, discussed the kids' day at school, then tucked them into bed as usual. She was about to turn on the radio so they could listen to Edward R. Murrow's broadcasts from London when Roger said, "Grace, don't turn that on just now. We need to talk."

Admitting guilt is a tricky thing. In the right place, to the right person — say in the church confessional to a priest — it's one thing, but in the living room to one's wife, it can be quite another. Roger stumbled through a progression of apologies before ever getting to the behavior that had brought them to this moment. Grace had to frequently inquire as to what he was actually trying to say. Euphemisms flowed from Roger's mouth like a kaleidoscope of butterflies taking wing. One would have to be extremely skilled in linguistics to get to the essence of the sordid behavior he was trying to wrap in a torrent of weasel words. Grace possessed such skill. When it became apparent that serial adultery was at the core of Roger's ramblings, Grace asked to be excused for just a moment. She stepped into the guest bathroom and vomited into the sink.

After a few minutes had passed, Grace returned and began a cross-examination that would wither the most expert witness. She wanted names, dates, locales, number of times, degree of satisfaction, use or non-use of appropriate protection, and perhaps most importantly to her... exactly who knew and who didn't know about Roger's degenerate deeds. That question led to the introduction of blackmail which Roger had yet to bring up.

Incredulous is perhaps too mild a word to describe Grace's reaction to the ransom being sought for keeping proof of Roger's contemptable comportment from public view. She was gobsmacked to think that any husband would ever ask his wife to entertain the thought of such a sin. Particularly with someone she'd never seen, didn't know, and probably couldn't be trusted to keep his end of the bargain. And to his credit, though he had virtually none left, Roger didn't ask. He simply reported the blackmailer's demand. Plus his admonition that he knew Grace would never consider such a thing and that he'd never allow it anyway. That last declaration was the proverbial bridge too far. "What?" she exclaimed. "You won't *allow*. Who the hell do you think you are? After what you've done to me... and this family... what makes you think you can allow or not allow anything." Hers was not a rhetorical question. Still, Roger had no answer for it.

That night didn't really end. The sun of the next day simply came up and found them still sitting in the living room bleary-eyed and bludgeoned with sadness and regret. Roger wasn't about to go to bed or take the shower that he badly needed without Grace's permission. She wasn't about to grant it. Eventually, however, she got up and went to their bedroom. He heard the door lock and knew further discussion at this time was futile. It was Friday. He'd simply go to work in the clothes and humiliation he was wearing.

THE LOBBY OF THE Drake Hotel on Saturday night buzzed with its usual swarm of guests, gadabouts, and gawkers. It was the place to see if one was a tourist and the place to be seen if one wanted to be chronicled in the society section of the *Sunday Tribune.* Porter was neither, but he was there to see if the seeds of his illicit endeavor were going to bear fruit. He selected a lounge chair that provided a perfect sightline to the building's front doors, as well as a three-hundred-and-sixty-degree view of the entire reception area. Porter was unconcerned about being spotted. Mrs. Gammon had no idea what he looked like and if Mr. Gammon was accompanying her, Porter would abort without incident.

The previous night, Roger had almost fallen off the couch he had been exiled to when Grace told him she had thought the whole thing over and that, for the good of their marriage, she was going to go through with it. Roger attempted to dissuade her, but she said her mind was made up. What was one repugnant physical debasement compared to the ongoing mental and emotional damage that would be visited upon them and their innocent children if the shame and embarrassment of Roger's disgusting womanizing were made public? Their family would be ostracized. Their name linked with ignominy. And Grace herself would be laughed at, talked about behind her back, and forever thought of as that dreadful little housewife who was not enough of a woman to satisfy her man. Yes, she would do it, she'd decided. She'd go alone to the hotel and room 401. But only for one hour. Roger was to wait and follow. If she hadn't come down from the room by 9 p.m., Roger was to come up and get her.

Porter, eyes glued to the front entrance, spied her as she strode through the door at 7:55. She looked magnetic. The picture of elegance in her high heels and fox coat. Her yellow hair shone like the moon. Her red lipstick and nails projected sophistication and allure simultaneously. Her stride was imperially confident with no hint of hesitation.

He was in awe. Porter had never had a woman like this before. Had never let himself dream of having one. There was the occasional shopgirl, or lovelorn spinster, and of course the prostitutes. But there had never been anyone like this. Such was his adoration that he gazed too longingly and almost missed crossing the lobby and stepping into the same elevator she was taking. "Four, please," she said to the elevator operator who then looked at Porter. He only nodded his head, indicating the same. The ride up was exhilarating. Her perfume filled the enclosure with hints of papaya. Upon reaching the fourth floor, Porter, still intoxicated by the aroma, almost forgot to step out after she did.

Grace checked the numbers on the doors and saw that the ones to her right started at 420 and began to decline. She immediately headed in that direction. Porter quickly exited the elevator and began attending to his tie that didn't need attention. When Grace arrived at 401 and raised her hand to rap on the door, Porter was a few feet behind her. He said, "No need to knock. I'll let us in." Initially startled, Grace hid her surprise well and merely stepped aside to let him unlock the door. He did so. Grace entered. Porter followed, then locked the door behind him.

"I brought some wine," he began, then naively continued, "wasn't sure whether you liked red or white, so I got both."

Grace glanced at the bottles and didn't recognize either of the cheap brands. She remarked derisively, "I don't require liquid courage. Do you?"

Unsure of how to respond, Porter stammered, "Well... no, not really. I mean, I just thought you might..."

"Are the negatives and prints here?" Grace asked abruptly.

"Yes, I have them. But you don't get them, well, until we..."

"Prove that you have them," Grace demanded.

Porter crossed to the dresser, pulled open one of the drawers, and removed a large envelope.

"Show me what's inside," she continued.

He took the photographs and the negatives out then spread them atop the dresser.

Grace looked at them but showed no emotion. She looked at Porter. "What is required of me?" she asked.

Porter realized the time had come. She was a cold bitch to be sure. But he sensed he was now in charge. "Why don't we start with this?" Porter suggested, pointing to the one of the photos of Roger being treated to fellatio from a nude brunette.

"All right," Grace said. "Why don't you sit in that chair?"

"Yes. Get comfortable. Good idea," Porter responded. He moved to the chair and sat. "Why don't you stand in front of me and start getting out of those clothes... slowly."

Grace's tone momentarily changed, she became demure. "Is that a radio? Can we have some music?"

"Sure," Porter answered. "Why not?" He reached over to the end table beside him, turned the knob on the radio and, to Grace's amazement, out came the melodious voices of Bing Crosby and the Andrews Sisters crooning the chorus of the novelty hit tune, *Pistol Packing Mama.* "Jesus, what are the odds," she couldn't keep from saying.

"What? What are you smiling about?" he asked.

Grace opened the purse she had with her and reached inside. When her hand came out, it was holding a Ruger .22 Caliber Semiautomatic. Porter was both shocked and addled as he tried to comprehend what he was seeing. Crosby's dulcet tones came through the radio singing, "Lay that pistol down, babe, lay that pistol down..."

"Turn it up," Grace said.

Porter started to shake his head no, but Grace pointed the gun at him and raised her voice. "Turn it up, I said. Loud!"

Porter did as he was told, realizing that perhaps he hadn't given enough thought to the potential downsides of his chosen vocation. Then suddenly, he came to the enlightened conclusion that it had all gone to shit, hadn't it? The night. His plan. His life. "Please," he began. "I won't..."

Grace could barely hear what he was saying. The music was too loud. Of course it wouldn't have mattered anyway. She planned to engage in no conversation before pumping two slugs into Porter's chest.

While a .22 is far from the kind of weapon a professional might choose for such a task, at such close range it was more than adequate. Looking down at his blood-stained shirt, unable to move, Porter made one last request. "Could you at least kiss me?" Grace shot him again for asking.

Fifty minutes later, as agreed, Roger was about to knock on the door of Room 401. As he was raising his hand, he could faintly hear the strains of *That Old Black Magic* coming from inside the room. Roger had no way of knowing what he would find when he came to retrieve Grace, but he certainly didn't expect to hear a Johnny Mercer tune wafting in the air. He knocked anyway and immediately heard Grace's voice. "Is that you, Roger?"

"Yes," he answered.

"Come on in, the door's unlocked." she said, as the volume of the music suddenly increased.

Roger stepped through the door and closed it behind him. He could see a man sitting in a chair across the room. A man who looked somewhat familiar. Roger sensed he had seen or met the man before, but he wasn't sure where? Was he sleeping? What were those red splotches on his white shirt? "Grace? Are you okay? Where are you?"

Roger took one step further into the room, stopping in front of the bathroom door. The door that Grace stepped through, raising the gun to Roger's temple and shooting him in the head.

As her husband lay on the plush carpet, Grace removed a floral embroidered white linen handkerchief from her purse. She used it to wipe her fingerprints off the Ruger before putting the pistol into Roger's dead hand. Then she took the negatives and all but two of the photographs, folded them, and crammed them into her purse, leaving the envelope and two of the less graphic pictures to indicate what had obviously transpired. A man had tried to blackmail her husband. He killed the depraved villain and then, overcome with guilt for what he had done to his wife and family, atoned by taking his own life. It would wash, she thought. The Drake certainly didn't want the publicity and so would push to keep the incident quiet. The police already had more crime on their hands than they had time to deal with. And Roger's company would definitely want to keep a low profile regarding such despicable goings-on with its own employees.

On her way out, Grace decided that even though there was a decided chill in the air, she would walk a bit before hailing a cab that would take her home. The crisp, cold air energized her as she reflected on her mastery of a situation that would have overwhelmed a lessor woman. That loathsome blackmailer certainly got what he deserved. And while Roger's demise was both appropriate and necessary, he did have his good points. That's why Grace would explain their father's passing to their daughters by praising him as a man who loved his family so much, that he was willing to commit the ultimate sacrifice to make sure they could all live without want. The million-dollar life insurance policy that the company had awarded Roger as one of their top executives would assure a pleasant and privileged future for them all. Yes, in reality, Roger was a pig, but a particularly productive one. Productive enough to rise through his company to a position of stature and authority in only two years. It had taken older, more experienced men much longer. Much longer than the two years it had taken Roger to... two years... the words stuck in her mind and held for a moment.

The last two days since Roger confessed had been a blur. Had it been only two days? It seemed so much longer. Two days... two years... what did Roger say about two years? "Oh, of course. I remember," she said out loud, her thoughts spilling into actual speech as others she passed on the sidewalk wondered who this strange woman was, talking to herself as she walked. "It was the insurance policy. He said it had a clause that keeps the company from having to pay if suicide is committed within two years. But those two years ended yesterday, right? April 1st. It is April, isn't it?"

An elderly black woman caught just the end of Grace's monologue and responded as she passed, "Can't get out of winter early, child. March got thirty-one days. It don't end til' tomorrow."

—THE END—

About the Author

Joe Kilgore is an award-winning author of novels, novellas, screenplays, and short stories. Ten of his novels have been published as well as a collection of short tales. Joe lives and writes in Austin, Texas. You can learn more about him and his work at joekilgore.com or follow him at x.com/JoeKilgore13.

The Day the FBI Came to the Door

By Ellen Byerrum

THE DAY THE FBI came to the door, I'd just put the children down for their naps.

I was still in the habit of watching them sleep — my girl and my boy — and kissing them softly on the tops of their heads. Their hair was as soft as duck down and their breathing the sigh of angels. A fierceness clenched my heart every time I looked at my sweet toddlers, and I swore no harm would ever touch them.

With housing almost impossible to find, even after the war, I knew how fortunate I was to live in our compact Del Ray bungalow, with small maple saplings out in front that would grow with us. How fortunate I was to tread on the dark red linoleum floor that I washed and waxed that morning, and how fortunate I was to fill the new General Electric refrigerator with fresh food. The mid-century was almost here and years of promise lay ahead. The privations of the war years seemed far away.

The day the FBI came to my door, it was a chilly March afternoon punctuated with harsh sharp winds and a blindingly blue sky. It was hard to remember the beautiful Virginia spring would be here soon. Yet although it was over, the war was never far from my thoughts.

Keeping me warm were my black cashmere sweater and my ruby-red wool circle skirt with black-and-white flecks. It amused me that my skirt and my lipstick matched the kitchen floor. My feet, covered with white ankle socks, were tucked into new penny loafers that sported shiny copper Lincolns. My auburn hair was neatly brushed back into a ponytail. The very picture of a satisfied modern homemaker. Yes, I could be a walking, talking magazine advertisement.

On the stove, the coffee had just finished percolating, filling the air with its rich aroma. I was about to pour a little canned milk into it when the doorbell rang. I set the can on the counter and strolled into the living room.

Before answering the bell, I peered through the sheer curtains to assess the visitors on my stoop: two crewcuts wearing gray suits, white shirts, and muted ties. I knew who they were because my neighbor Irma was a friendly gossip. Big-boned and bighearted, she was very good at repeating raw information. Irma had no filters. Once a fact went in, it immediately poured out of her. I found that sometimes wearing, sometimes useful. And she had a heart of gold. Did I mention that?

Just this week, Irma reported that the Federal Bureau of Investigation ("of all things!") was in the neighborhood, asking questions about other neighbors, prying into everybody's business. She hadn't had a visit herself yet, but she had this on good information. She couldn't wait.

"Communists! Can you imagine?" Irma said. "I mean to tell you, why would Communists want to live here? In this neighborhood? Don't they all want to go live in the godforsaken Soviet Union where they can all think alike and dress alike and look alike and eat borscht or something? I certainly don't think we have any Communists here. I'd know."

I was sure she would. I told her I had no idea. I hadn't met any neighborhood Communists myself.

"I mean to tell you, Harold says he can smell the Reds. And if there were Reds here, he'd be the first to know."

I assured her Harold had impeccable instincts for that kind of thing.

"Yes?" I opened the door a crack. The lead crewcut flashed a badge and I studied it. It was the genuine article.

"FBI, Ma'am. May we come in?"

"Yes, of course." Was I supposed to say *no*?

I put on my gracious smile and opened the door wider, glancing at their shoes, hoping they wouldn't track dirt onto my clean carpet. I relaxed; both pairs were polished to a bright shine and the agents wiped them on the welcome mat before stepping inside. They were well trained.

The lead agent introduced himself as Agent Johnson. His companion was Agent Daly. Johnson was blond and stockier than the brown-haired Daly, but both had bright blue eyes.

Were they regulation Government Issue, I wondered? Stamped out of a mold? Healthy, husky, and polite?

"Would you care for coffee?" I asked. "It's fresh."

Johnson replied that they had drunk a lot of coffee already. I smiled at that. If they'd been sipping all my neighbors' high-test java, they would be climbing the walls. Perhaps I should have suggested martinis to take the edge off their professional rigidity?

"Won't you sit down?" I indicated the immaculate-though-small living room where Jake and I entertained company. "If you don't mind, I'm going to get myself some while it's hot."

The agents remained standing until I returned with my cup and saucer and sat down in my favorite turquoise chair. They took both ends of the cream-colored sofa, perched on the edge and sitting up rod-straight.

"How can I help you? The FBI doesn't come to my door every day. Or any day. Is there trouble in the neighborhood?" I'm sure I seemed ever-so-flustered. I wasn't.

"I'll keep this short, Mrs.—?" Johnson said.

It was nice of him to ask, though if they were any kind of FBI agents, I was pretty sure they already knew my name.

"It's Mitchell, Catherine Mitchell. My friends call me Cat. My husband is at work." I assumed they also knew that Jake worked at the State Department, shoveling paper. It was good steady work.

"Let me get to the point, Mrs. Mitchell. These are tense times in the world. We all like to think that the war has ended, but—" He paused for effect. "There's another war going on now, a Cold

War. We have information that one of your neighbors might be dabbling in the Communist Party."

I made sure to gasp. "No! Not really?"

Since the war, and even before, the government was on the hunt for the Red Menace. But in this country, who and what was this menace? A handful of elite screenwriters and other wealthy Hollywood types playing at communism? They didn't frighten me. I hadn't noticed them sharing their worldly goods, so how committed could they be? They seemed to want everybody else to fall in with the party line. I imagined they would come to their senses sooner or later.

On the other hand, when they were trying to steal information on national security and our atomic secrets, I was pretty hard-nosed. I'd had firsthand knowledge of Soviet methods. Their brutal brand of communism alarmed me, as well as the resulting East German style of totalitarianism.

"Communists here? No! I had no idea. Who?" I opened my eyes wide and leaned forward in my chair, encouraging them to continue. They clearly thought I was simply a housewife, and quite possibly, a simpleton. It was obvious these FBI agents had no idea what I did during the war. My record with the Office of Strategic Services was, and would continue to be, sealed.

"Do you know a Mrs. Frieda Becker? Next block over," Johnson said. "Dirty blonde. Attractive. A little older than you, Ma'am. German national."

Attractive? I didn't think so.

"Frieda Becker?" *So that was what she was calling herself these days.* "I may have seen her in the neighborhood, but we've not met yet. Surely, she's not... one of *them*?" I didn't want to overplay my little act, so I pulled it back a bit.

Irma had filled me in on the newcomer just the week before, when a moving van pulled up and deposited some paltry possessions at one of the plainer little houses on the next street over. At the first opportunity, Irma had taken the new neighbor some brownies. She only knew that the woman was German and named Frieda. Irma wasn't inclined to trust her just yet. She'd have to see if the woman returned her brownie pan. It was one of Irma's character tests.

I had spotted this new neighbor myself just yesterday at the corner grocery, from behind the five-foot-tall bright-yellow display of Velveeta cheese. You know, the creamier cheese. "Frieda" didn't notice me. I recognized her immediately. Some people you never forget. I picked up an orange-yellow package of processed cheese and counted my items, taking time to consider what her sudden appearance in America could mean. Here, in this sleepy suburb of Washington, D.C., near the epicenter of the free world. I had to calm the thrill of danger I felt, and my racing pulse. Still, I had to be sure it was the same woman.

"Mrs. Becker, Frieda, says she's a German refugee seeking asylum. Says she has family here, seems to have a job in the District." Agent Johnson broke into my thoughts. "But we have some pretty good information about her underground activities with known Reds." He nodded his head as he said it, wanting me to nod mine in silent agreement. I nodded.

"What kind of underground activities?" I asked.

"That's classified." He replied exactly as I expected him to.

Frieda's real name was Ava Faust. Apparently Agent Johnson didn't know that. When I'd spotted her in the grocery store, Ava appeared much diminished since I had first known her. She didn't look as smug or sure of herself in a shabby gray coat with a drab scarf tied underneath her chin. It could have been an act. She could be trying to be invisible. Her hair was darker than the platinum halo she first sported, but the eyes were just the same, small, ice blue, and calculating. Yet it was the distinct V-shaped scar on her forehead that identified her unmistakably. The puckered scar left from a bullet that unfortunately missed killing her.

As far as I knew, Frieda Becker — or Ava Faust — was no Communist. She was just a grasping amoral opportunist. If she was now a Red, or posing as a Red, it was some game she was playing. Perhaps the FBI could tell me.

"What would you do with her?" I asked. "If this information turns out to be true?" I rattled my cup in the saucer, ever so slightly, for nervous effect.

"Depends on what she's doing here, Ma'am. Deport her, at the very least. Perhaps even prison."

"Do you think she's a *spy*?" This entire area was a snake's nest of spies of all stripes, spies who wanted to know what went on in America's capital city. I thought it highly likely that Ava Faust was now a spy. But for whom?

"I can't comment on that, Mrs. Mitchell."

"Cat," I prompted him.

"Perhaps you've been watching too many movies, Mrs.— Cat." Johnson smiled for my benefit.

Agent Daly chuckled reassuringly. "We don't draw conclusions," he said, making it clear he thought she was as Red as the red planet Mars.

I allowed myself to laugh a little. "Perhaps you're right."

He rattled on for a bit about how the FBI was on the job, protecting the USA from all our enemies, foreign and domestic. My thoughts were on Ava.

———

LISETTE WARNED ME IT would be dangerous, all those years ago — 1940. I didn't care. How dangerous could it be? She made it sound like a great adventure. America hadn't even entered the war yet, but it would eventually. It was only a matter of time.

A natural-born leader, Lisette was dark-haired, pretty, and brash. So very *Parisienne.* She could cajole or bully anyone into going her way. She wore her passion for freedom like a scarlet dress, where everyone could see it. In the end, she miscalculated.

The Germans were on the march and they would be in Paris soon, she told me. There was nothing that could stop them. However, I could be of help to her and others who resisted the Nazi onslaught. If I accompanied her on her missions to relay information, we would be just two students on a jaunt, touring the city, trying to find a bit more bread or cheese or wine. Everyone knew that students were always hungry.

"You look so *Americaine,* Cat," she would always say, as if it were a surprise. "Really, no one will ever know our little secret." She meant I looked naïve and clueless, the perfect cover.

It would be a lark, she added. Just think of the stories I would be able to tell one day, one day when the war was over and the Germans were gone.

Before I met Lisette, I was studying in Paris at the university, trying to learn the language of my French grandmother, who at that time was in Illinois intruding on my parents, drinking wine, and baffling everyone but my mother with her impenetrable accent. My French was still poor, yet improving. Later, my French became very good indeed.

I fell in love with the City of Light because that's what everybody did. How could we help it? We students gathered in coffee shops. We debated for hours. We drank coffee and wine. From Lisette, I learned about subjects not covered in my textbooks — including the encroaching gray threat of the Nazis, the *Boche*. I saw what they did to people, how they murdered the spirit. I heard much more. I was not a spy, not at that point. I was just along for the ride. Until my last ride with Lisette.

The mission went well, at first. She delivered her information to her male contact, and sometime lover, as we sipped a bottle of wine. They excused themselves and I am still glad they had those last few minutes to themselves, to make love one final time. Afterward, we said our goodbyes and left the café. One minute we were strolling down a cobbled side street. The next, grabbed from behind, hoods placed over our heads. We were picked up and thrown in the back of a truck. Struggling only brought blows. We were slumped side-by-side on a wooden bench that jarred me every time the truck hit a bump or a rock in the road. The constricted space smelled of oil and dirt, and men. They spoke in guttural foreign accents and occasionally they laughed. At us, I assumed.

I was dazed and we didn't try to speak. At one point, Lisette found my hand and squeezed it to comfort me, to give me strength. A brief moment, but I'll never forget it. When I need courage, I think of that moment, and Lisette's bravery. I took a deep breath and no matter what happened, promised I would be brave and never disgrace myself, or her.

The truck drove for what seemed like an hour or more, careening around corners, which forced me to hold onto the bench, jabbing splinters into my hands. It finally slammed to a stop, sending us to the floor. Again, hands grabbed us and hauled us out of the truck.

Were they going to shoot us?

Rough hands pulled me through the cold street, across a doorway and into a warm room. I heard dishes clattering and voices speaking in another room but couldn't make out the conversation. We must have been in the back of a café. An aroma of bread and spilled wine and sharp cheese hung in the air, reminding me I hadn't eaten since early that morning. I wouldn't eat again for another day.

The hood was yanked roughly off my face. It took a moment of blinking to adjust to the light and the reality of the hated gray uniforms that surrounded us. They tied our hands behind us. The knots could have been tighter, but I was glad they weren't.

I gazed at my surroundings. The floor was brick, the walls plaster. We were in a kitchen of some small bistro. It was there where I got my first look at Ava Faust. Later I learned she was the mistress of a high-ranking Nazi and enjoyed helping him with his work. She enjoyed killing too, perhaps more than he did, or so I was told. He let her question us in the company of some soldiers. She spoke French, presumably better than her Nazi lover.

My first glimpse of Ava revealed a black widow spider in the center of a half-dozen gray uniforms. She wore an expensive black tailored dress with shiny gold buttons. Three-quarter-length sleeves showed off the tinkling bracelet she wore: small, square mother-of-pearl boxes linked together with rubies. The rubies matched her dark nails, which she had filed to sharp points. Scarlet high-heeled shoes made her look taller than she was. And of course, her hair was that particular brand of Aryan blond touted so often in German propaganda. Her narrow azure eyes seemed to gleam with pleasure at the sight of two rabbits caught in her trap.

I focused on the scar on her forehead, memorizing its size and shape and color. She didn't like that, and she brushed her hair down over the mark.

"Don't look at me," she screamed at us in French.

I said nothing. She asked us questions that I couldn't answer and to which Lisette refused to respond. All I could say, over and over, was that I knew nothing, but my poor French and my accent told her I was American.

"I don't like your attitude," she said. "I don't like you."

Did she think I liked her?

At one point, she slapped my face, scraping those sharpened nails across my cheek. I could feel the sting and the warm blood running down my face.

Lisette was not as lucky as I. Ava screamed and slapped and punched her repeatedly. I swallowed the desire to scream back. Lisette had warned me if we were ever apprehended, to show no fear, to never cry or scream. I concentrated on the bracelet that caught the light, and I worked my fingers to untie the rope around my hands.

"Tell me, you slut. I know everything," she yelled again at Lisette. "I convinced your lover to talk." Lisette didn't flinch. "But he will talk no more."

Lisette said nothing. Ava nodded to a soldier who left the room and soon we heard gunshots. There was no way to know whether it was all a ruse. Still, Lisette refused to talk, refused to cry, refused to break.

Quick as flicking a switchblade, Ava opened one of the pearled squares of the bracelet and withdrew a petite pellet. She held it up like a rare diamond. I didn't know at first what it was. She reclosed the pearl door.

"Tell me what you know, French slut," Ava yelled in Lisette's face.

"I know you are the devil from Hell, *boche*," Lisette spat back at Ava. Her last words.

With two guards holding Lisette down, Ava forced her mouth open and held it shut until her prey bit the cyanide pellet. Lisette fell to the ground, writhing, agony in her eyes. It was over quickly, and the light that was Lisette was extinguished.

I knew I was next. I said my prayers.

Turning to me, Ava dragged her nails across my face again and stared hard, breathing fast. "Unfortunately, I am instructed to let you go as a warning. Do not play at spy games. If I ever see you again, I will kill you, stupid American girl."

Something hard grew inside me, like impenetrable barbed wire around my heart. My hands were now free, waiting.

"Not if I kill you first, you German viper."

I went crazy. With everything I had, I sprang up and head-butted her in the stomach. We both fell to the floor, and to my satisfaction I heard one of her high heels snap. She couldn't breathe for a moment. I continued pummeling her face. She wasn't prepared for my fury. I ripped the sparkling bracelet from her wrist and heard it clatter to the floor. I bit her face, drawing blood. I tried to tear her ear off.

We were separated by two soldiers before I could inflict further injury. One pointed his pistol at me, but the other stopped him. "*Nicht die Amerikanische,*" the soldier said.

Two of them had to hold Ava away from me. She spat her venom like a crazed snake. Her carefully styled hair was all undone and I had bloodied her nose. That was some small satisfaction.

Even though America hadn't joined the war yet, I was stunned they spared me. The soldiers retied my hands, much harder this time, and put the hood back over my head. They hustled me out to the sound of Ava howling for them to find her bracelet, her precious, deadly piece of jewelry. With my face covered by the hood, my eyes full of tears for poor Lisette, I smiled.

I returned to America shortly thereafter and finished my studies. As soon as I could, I joined the OSS and became an operative. They were happy to have a complete description of the Nazi bitch who had killed more than one resistance fighter. The OSS were never able to find Ava Faust. But I never gave up hope that one day we would meet again.

More than that, I cannot say, even in a private memoir.

I SIPPED MY COFFEE and looked up at agents Johnson and Daly. "I'm sorry I can't be of more help." I smiled. "And she really might be deported?" I wondered how much time I had.

"It's a possibility," Johnson said. "We don't need to import them, we have enough of our own Commies."

I didn't want Ava Faust deported. I didn't want her tied up in red tape. I wanted her dead.

Friendly Agent Johnson was useful to me and I was thankful. He confirmed that "Frieda Becker" was a German refugee under investigation by the FBI. She was "playing around," he said, in the Communist Party. I considered it likely she was sent here to retrieve secrets for some Soviet overlords. And now the filthy little war criminal was conveniently living on the next block. Very stupid of her not to know everyone in the neighborhood.

Johnson and Daly seemed satisfied that I had nothing to offer their investigation. I was just another small-town wife and mother, naïve and completely shocked at this threat infiltrating her quiet neighborhood.

"Thank you, Ma'am." Johnson gave me a card with a phone number on it. "If you think of something, or notice something, you will call me, won't you?"

"You can depend on it," I answered.

I shut the door and watched them leave from the living room windows. They seemed bored. The lead agent shook his head and slapped his notebook shut. I had played my part well and gave myself a passing grade.

After their black Ford disappeared down East Randolph Avenue, I walked into our light blue bedroom, opened my jewelry box and removed the false bottom. I carefully withdrew a bracelet with seven mother-of-pearl blocks, connected by rubies. I dangled it in the light.

How did it wind up with me and not Ava?

I have always been quick with my hands. After I jumped on her and ripped off the bitch's bracelet, I rolled on top of her and scooped it up while I was beating her face, tucking it into my skirt. She didn't notice it was missing until I was being marched away. From her squealing, I gathered the bracelet had some sentimental value. It also had six more cyanide pellets. I eventually used five in the service of my country.

You would never think I could get away with it — reentering the country wearing that bracelet on my wrist. It looked expensive, like something that should be declared. The agent at customs remarked suspiciously that it was very pretty and asked me where it came from. I don't know why I said "Iowa," and that it had belonged to my mother. He nodded and cautioned me against taking something valuable and flashy like that into another country. Not that I'd be going back to Europe anytime soon, because we were living in troubled times.

I always planned to get rid of the last remaining cyanide pellet, turn it in, before the children started rummaging into things they shouldn't.

The day the FBI came to the door, that bracelet went into the deep pocket of my red circle skirt, where I could feel it bounce against my thigh.

The children would wake up soon from their naps, so I called my friend Irma, explaining I had forgotten a few things at the store. Would she mind coming over for an hour to watch the kids? I had a nice new LIFE magazine she could look through. Of course, she said yes. She was one of those solid, dependable women, even though she was afraid of Communists. I made a note to remember to pick up a cinnamon coffee cake at the grocery store to thank her.

My black speckled swing coat was hanging by the front door, with a matching scarf. I slipped the wrap over my shoulders. The hall mirror told me I looked like a respectable middle-class young mother. I smiled at my reflection. I jingled the bracelet in my pocket and opened my front door.

It was time to clean up the neighborhood.

—THE END—

About the Author

Mystery and thriller writer Ellen Byerrum is a former journalist who worked in Washington, D.C., as well as a produced and published playwright. In addition to her recent Art Deco Mysteries — award-winning *Crook Tales for Two* and, coming soon, *These Crooked Things* — she is the author of the Lacey Smithsonian Crime of Fashion Mysteries, two of which were filmed for Lifetime.

In the interest of research, she studied for and received her private investigator's registration for the Commonwealth of Virginia. She has also researched haunted clothing at the Smithsonian Costume Collections, toured a dying velvet factory in Virginia, and interviewed a host of experts for her books.

In addition to adult mysteries, Byerrum pens plays and has written a children's picture book, *Sherlocktopus Holmes: Eight Arms of the Law*; a middle school mystery, *The Children Didn't See Anything*; and numerous short stories.

You can find her on Facebook and Instagram, or at her website: www.ellenbyerrum.com.

Box of Memories

By Bruce H. Markuson

I WAS SITTING IN the dining room at the retirement home when my granddaughter walked in holding a box with EMMY MORRISON written on it. Morrison was my maiden name, and no one has called me "Emmy" in decades.

"Hi Grandma," my granddaughter said. "Listen, someone left this on the front porch and there was a note with it that says:

> Dear Emma,
> Hi, long time no see. My mother recently passed away. While cleaning out her house I came across this box my brother had. It was buried deep in the attic. I thought you might like it.
> Rachael Bloomberg"

"Rachael Bloomberg, now there's a name I haven't heard in a long time. Oh, my..." My voice trailed off.

"Grandma, what is it?"

"She's David Bloomberg's sister."

"Who?"

"David was an old, old boyfriend of mine."

"Boyfriend?" my granddaughter abruptly said.

"Now, dear, this was long before I met your grandfather. Rest his soul."

"Should we open it?" she asked.

"By all means."

First, she pulled out a photograph of me wearing love beads and a leather tasseled bikini top. There was a peace symbol painted on my face.

"Grandma, is that you?"

"Well, believe it or not, I was once a young lady like you."

"And who is that?" She pointed to the young man whose lap I was sitting on in the photograph.

"That, my dear, was David."

"I see he didn't have long hair."

"No, no he didn't. He was in the Army."

She pulled out a few more photos. "Wow, Grandma. You were at Woodstock. Groovy."

"Four hundred thousand people showed up at Woodstock. And, yes, David and I were there, and we never used the word, 'groovy.'"

Reaching into the box again, my granddaughter said, "What are these plastic things labeled Janis Joplin, Peter, Paul and Mary, and the Beatles?"

"Those, my dear, are 8-track tapes. The predecessor to Spotify."

"This is *not* what I think it is!" my granddaughter said loudly enough for all the nursing home to hear as she pulled out a small plastic bag containing a few joints and other drug paraphernalia. It seemed everyone in the room was staring at us. Quickly, I took the bag, crumpled it up, and looked for a garbage can behind me to throw it in.

"The Sixties were kind of a radical time," I explained. "And, yes, we smoked marijuana and did some LSD. Dear, just promise me you won't follow my bad example."

When I turned back, my granddaughter was reading one of my love letters. "Grandma," she commented, "these letters are really hot and heavy. Mom always said you had a boyfriend before Grandpa, but that who he was has always been a mystery."

Quickly, I covered the letters with my hand and politely took them from her. "Dear, the Sixties was also the time of the Sexual Revolution. And now you know why my old boyfriend was always a mystery. That was something I wanted to keep from your grandfather."

"So, what happened with David?" my granddaughter asked.

"He was going to work some cushy desk job at the Pentagon. His father pulled some strings and had him set up to be some assistant to a colonel or something. But it was the Sixties. I wanted him to leave the army. I thought the war was wrong. I had to protest. We got into a big fight about it. Then, after our big fight, after we broke up, he got upset. He said he had to go and do what they called 'getting his ticket punched.' So instead of serving at the Pentagon, he went to Vietnam."

"And he never came back?" my granddaughter guessed as she pulled a small container out of the box.

"No. No, he never came back."

I was silent for a moment, then I explained: "I would have stayed with him. He would have worked at the Pentagon, and my life would have been very different. But no, he was a military man. And I was just his hippy girlfriend." I wiped a tear from my eye and continued, "I always wondered how he felt. If only! If only he could have shown me that he was serious about the two of us."

My granddaughter just stared down at the small box she held in her hand.

"Dear? Dear, what is it?" I asked.

"Grandma!" she said as she turned the box around.

And there, nestled against a velvet background, I saw it: the box held an engagement ring.

—THE END—

About the Author

Bruce Markuson lives with his wife and two children in Milwaukee, Wisconsin. He is the author of a novel, *Wolf Spy,* as well as over 150 short stories. Bruce is currently working on several series. He enjoys writing and often finds himself with writer's obsession. He says the best way to write is to have an ending, then write to that ending.

Under the Proctor Street Bridge

By Michael Bracken

THERE IS SO MUCH I know now that I didn't understand during the summer of 1971. I was thirteen then, soon to start ninth grade at Mason Junior High School, and I spent most days with Tommy O'Connor, the third of seven children — and the only boy — living in a three-bedroom house across the street from the home I shared with my widowed father. The Vietnam War was winding down, Richard Nixon was running for re-election, and many teenaged veterans were more than a year away from voting in their first presidential election following the July passage of the 26th Amendment.

I didn't pay much attention to the news, and Tommy's mother wouldn't let him and his sisters watch it for fear they might learn what their father was doing halfway around the world and why people spit on him and other soldiers when they returned home.

As the only boys on the block, Tommy and I quickly became friends after I moved to Tacoma that summer. I had arrived with only what would fit in my father's AMC Rambler, so I had all my clothing and a few of my books, but I'd had to leave everything else behind, including my bicycle. Tommy didn't have much, either, and our detached garage, reached via the alley behind our house, became a repository for the junk Tommy and I accumulated that summer, which included broken toys we found in trash bins.

Tommy had freckles and a flattop so short it was difficult to tell his auburn hair was almost red. My dark hair was longer, over my collar and constantly falling into my eyes, but not because I followed the fashion sense of the day. My father just hadn't taken me to a barber since my mother's death. Our summer uniform was white undershirts, cut-off blue jeans, and sneakers. I wore a Howdy Doody wristwatch my mother had given me when I was younger, and I kept a house key on a chain around my neck. Tommy didn't need a key because there was always someone at his house, but he did wear a Saint Christopher medal received from his father for his confirmation.

When we had pocket change, which wasn't often, Tommy and I rode the bus to Point Defiance Park, where we ogled sunbathing girls, or we rode the bus downtown to visit the candle shops, funky clothing stores, and head shops where hippies and war-scarred young veterans hung out. Most of our adventures, though, were limited to how far we could walk and still return home in time for dinner. Sometimes we went all the way to the shopping district at North 26th Street and North Proctor Street to visit the Western Auto, where we took our time examining the various Western Flyer bicycles on display and assuring the young blonde behind the counter, who was not much older than Tommy's oldest sister, that we were saving up to buy our own.

Our favorite place to go, though, was Puget Gulch. When we had an entire day to kill, we hiked the length of the gulch from Monroe Street at the upper end all the way down to the waterfront, keeping close to the muddy banks of Puget Creek. More often we stayed under or near the Proctor Street bridge, poking through the things people dumped into the gulch. We found discarded appliances, car parts, and one day, while nosing around in the undergrowth on the north side of the gulch, a bicycle frame. We carried it home and put it in the garage behind my house, hoping to find some wheels, a seat, and handlebars so we could assemble our own Frankenstein bicycle. We didn't say anything to anyone — not even a few weeks later when we found another bicycle frame — because my father had taught me the rule of finders keepers.

We didn't often see other people in the gulch, and we usually avoided them when we did. Tommy's mother said hippies and homeless people camped in the gulch and that we should avoid them because you never knew what they might do.

WHEN WE WEREN'T ROAMING Tacoma's North End during the day, Tommy and I hung out at his house. His mother often made us sandwiches and asked questions about my parents, usually when peanut butter was stuck to the roof of my mouth and made responding difficult. One day when Tommy's sisters were outside and just the three of us sat at their kitchen table, she said, "It must be hard, not having a mother."

"Yeah," I said. "I guess. I try not to think about it."

"I know my Tommy misses his father."

"But he ain't dead, is he?"

She smiled wanly. "Sometimes I think he might as well be, as little as we see of him."

"Mom!" Tommy had told me all about his father, a master sergeant serving his third year-long tour of duty in Vietnam. Tommy barely knew his father because the man only came home for a brief time between each tour. "You don't really mean that, do you?"

Mrs. O'Connor ignored him. "I'll bet your father gets lonely."

"I don't know," I said. "We never talk about it."

There was a faraway look in her eyes. Before she could ask another question, one of Tommy's younger sisters came running into the kitchen, crying because she had fallen and scraped her knee.

Another day, Tommy's mother asked what my father did, and I told her he worked smelting copper for American Smelting and Refining Company in Ruston, a small town surrounded on three sides by Tacoma and on the fourth by Puget Sound. The smelter was one of the possible sources of the aroma of Tacoma, an odor that often permeated the city back then.

"That's hard work," she said. She was standing at her living room window watching my father mow our yard, his shirt off.

There were several times I caught her staring out their front window, watching my father working in our yard, and I didn't understand her fascination with him. Though I didn't realize it then, my father was an attractive man in his mid-thirties, with thick black hair and a muscular build from years of backbreaking labor.

One Saturday, when Tommy's mother had all the girls in the family's 1965 Chevrolet Impala station wagon for a trip to the Fort Lewis PX, Tommy and I were sitting on the porch watching as she turned the ignition key. Nothing happened. She tried again and again. When it failed to start after many attempts, she leaned forward to rest her head on the steering wheel. I wasn't certain, but I thought she was crying.

"Hey, Mrs. O'Connor," I called from the porch, "let me get my dad."

I ran across the street, found my shirtless father in the backyard building a fence from discarded pallets, and told him what had happened. He grabbed his toolbox from the garage and followed me across the street. I introduced the two of them.

"Maggie," she said with a smile, after I introduced her as Mrs. O'Connor.

"David," he said. "Or Dave. Either one is fine."

She wet her lips with the tip of her tongue, and I realized at that moment that I had never seen her wearing lipstick before that day. They stared at each other until I interrupted. "Well?"

My father opened the station wagon's hood, poked around, and had her try again. The Impala started immediately. He closed the hood, walked back to the driver's window, and leaned against the station wagon with one hand on the door. She placed one of her hands on top of his and thanked him more than once.

When she finally drove away, I asked, "What was it?"

"Loose battery cable," he said. He was watching the station wagon disappear around the corner, not looking at me. "I cleaned the posts and tightened up the cables."

THAT EVENING, TOMMY'S MOTHER crossed the street carrying a foil-topped casserole dish captured between two oven mitts, and my father opened the door to her after she tapped the doorbell. She said, "I hope you haven't eaten yet. I made a hamburger casserole for you."

"You didn't have to do that." He stepped aside and let her into our house.

She carried the casserole into our kitchen and placed it on the stove.

"We haven't had a home-cooked meal in ages," he said. I almost reminded him that I had eaten with Tommy's family several times.

"You must miss your wife."

"I do," my father said, "more than I care to admit. What about you? Do you miss your husband?"

She nodded as they stared into each other's eyes.

I was hungry and the aroma of the hamburger casserole made my stomach growl. "Can we eat already?"

My father glanced at me. "Go ahead, Mikey. Serve yourself. I'll be back in a minute."

He took Mrs. O'Connor's elbow, led her to the door, and followed her onto the porch. Instead of serving myself dinner, I stood at the living room window and watched my father watch her cross the street to her own home.

Our next-door neighbor was standing on the sidewalk outside our house. "Be careful," he told my father. "You don't want people getting the wrong idea."

"What's that?"

"Her husband being away and you without a wife."

My father glared at him and returned to the house.

We ate the hamburger casserole for dinner, and it was good.

———————

THE AROMA OF TACOMA was particularly strong the day Tommy and I found a paper lunch sack filled with money beneath the Proctor Street bridge. We might have ignored it as someone's discarded lunch, but the bag had broken open and the green spilling from it wasn't lettuce. We had been hoping to a find a bicycle part or two, but the realization that we had found money instead made us stop our search.

Tommy held the bag and stared at me. "What should we do?"

"Finders keepers," I told him, parroting what my father said whenever we found loose change or wrinkled dollar bills on the ground.

"But—"

I took the bag from his hand, settled onto a bent and rusted bumper we often used as a bench, and counted the money. It was more than either of us had ever seen, and we knew what we wanted to do with it.

We walked to the Western Auto and examined all the bicycles on display. We knew we had to choose from those on display because we had no way to take unassembled bicycles home. So, Tommy chose the Fast One Buzz Bike with Billy Bar handlebars and saddle seat, I chose the 2+1 Buzz Bike with a wheelie bar extra wheel at the rear, and we selected a pair of bicycle combination locks. We took everything to the blonde at the counter.

"Finally saved up enough money?" she asked.

Before Tommy could say anything, I said, "Yes, ma'am."

"I look old enough to be a ma'am?"

"Yes, ma'am."

She laughed, rang up our purchase, and watched carefully as I counted out the money.

We wheeled our new bicycles outside, climbed on, and spent the rest of the day bicycling all over the North End, stopping once at 7-Eleven when we grew hungry and thirsty. When the afternoon turned into evening, we returned home, parked the bicycles in my garage, and went to Tommy's house for meatless spaghetti and garlic toast made with Wonder Bread. We watched television with his sisters while his mother washed dishes, and then I went home. My father was working second shift that day, so I was alone with some library books and a pitcher of grape Kool-Aid.

I WAS ASLEEP WHEN my father stormed into the house and woke me. Before I could say anything, he demanded, "Where'd you get the bicycles?"

"Finders keepers, Dad."

"Some kids left bicycles in their yard, and you took them?"

"We wouldn't do that," I insisted. "We bought them at Western Auto."

"Bought them? How? Where did you get that kind of money?"

I told him about finding the lunch sack full of cash, but he didn't believe me until I retrieved it from my room. He spread the remaining currency on the dining room table and counted it. When he finished, he looked at me. "There's eight hundred and twelve dollars here."

"And forty-three cents," I said as I removed the change from my pocket and put it on top of the currency. I added the Western Auto receipt for the bicycles and the receipt from 7-Eleven where we stopped for Slurpees and Snickers bars while we were riding all over the North End.

"I want you to show me exactly where you found this."

"Now?"

"Now. Get dressed."

While I was dressing, he called Tommy's mother and told her about the money and the new bicycles. I couldn't hear what she said, but a few minutes later Tommy knocked on our door. My father grabbed a high-powered flashlight before the three of us piled into our Rambler and drove to the Proctor Street bridge. He parked on the north end of the bridge because he didn't know that the path from Monroe Street was longer but easier, and he followed us down a steep path until we reached the bottom of the gulch where all the stuff tossed over the side of the bridge usually landed. As we approached the bottom, the putrid aroma of Tacoma grew stronger.

Streetlight and moonlight barely reached the bottom of the gulch through the tangle of trees and the shadow of the bridge. My father switched on his flashlight and began playing the light over a refrigerator, a washing machine, various car parts, and much more. I directed his attention to the spot where we'd found the lunch bag, and I showed him the car bumper we'd sat on while we counted the money before walking to the Western Auto.

While we waited, he walked all around the gulch-bottom junkyard until he found what we hadn't looked for earlier that day — a dead man wearing muddy boots, bellbottom jeans, a dirty undershirt, and a green fatigue jacket — and we realized that we weren't smelling just the city's putrid odor but the aroma of death. His head looked like it had been bashed in, and nearby was another bicycle frame, the third we'd seen at the bottom of the gulch. The body had been there long enough that insects and rodents had been at it, and my father was careful when he removed dog tags on a ball-chain necklace from around the dead man's neck.

"Up," my father said once he had the dog tags in hand. "Back to the top. We need to call the police."

The pharmacy two blocks north of the bridge had a pay phone out front. My father called the police to tell them what we had found, and he called Tommy's mother to tell her we wouldn't be home any time soon.

And we weren't.

While we waited, my father insisted we return the money, despite my protests. "But, Dad, you always say 'finders' keepers'."

"This kind of money wasn't lost," he explained. "It was stolen. It had to have been. And even if you didn't steal something, you have no right to keep something someone else stole."

A police cruiser arrived and then other first responders who secured the scene and dealt with the body and its removal from the gulch. My father gave a pair of plainclothes detectives the dead man's dog tags and the remaining money, along with the receipts for what we had purchased. They asked us question after question after question. They wanted to know how we'd found the money and how we'd brought my father back to the gulch and how he'd found the body.

The police used the dog tags to identify the dead man — a homeless Vietnam veteran who had been living in the gulch and who had burglarized a convenience store the previous night, taking nearly a thousand dollars from the office. He had been killed when the frame of a stolen bicycle thrown over the side of the bridge smashed the top of his head, causing him to fling the bag of cash several feet away.

The police later matched the bicycle frame's serial number to a theft report a few days old, and fingerprints on the frame led them to a pair of thieves who had been on a months-long spree, stealing bicycles and stripping them of easily repurposed parts. They also matched the serial numbers of the two frames Tommy and I had retrieved from the gulch to other theft reports and returned them to the rightful owners, even though the stripped frames were of little use without wheels and seats and handlebars.

The owner of the convenience store was willing to let Tommy and I keep the bicycles as a reward, but my father refused. He worked out a repayment plan and promised Tommy and I that he was going to put us to work to repay every cent of what we had taken.

We didn't know all of that the next morning when the police finally let us go and my father drove us home. He parked the Rambler in the garage next to our two new bicycles. As we headed across the street to tell Tommy's mother what had happened, we saw a green Army sedan parked in front of Tommy's house.

Standing on the porch with Tommy's mother was an Army officer and a chaplain, and just as we reached the porch, they notified her of her husband's death in Vietnam and how they were sorry for her loss. Her knees buckled, but by then my father was standing next to her, and he and the chaplain caught her.

The officer and the chaplain remained long enough to ensure that Tommy's mother would be okay, with my father reassuring them that he would take care of her, help with the children, notify relatives, and all the other things required in that situation. After they left, he held her as she cried into his shoulder.

After several minutes, she looked up into my father's eyes, and he kissed her forehead.

LATER, TOMMY AND I would grow our hair long, string our own love beads, and protest the war that had taken his father's life. Over the years, we would experience love and loss. We would lose my father and his mother and some of his sisters. But as the summer of 1971 ended, we understood that our lives had changed forever.

—THE END—

About the Author

Michael Bracken is an Edgar Award and Shamus Award nominee and three-time Derringer Award winner. The author of more than thirteen hundred short stories, his crime fiction has appeared in *The Best American Mystery Stories*, *The Best Mystery Stories of the Year*, and many other publications. Additionally, Bracken is the editor of *Black Cat Mystery Magazine* and editor or co-editor of three dozen anthologies, including a Derringer Award winner and three Anthony Award nominees. He is a recipient of the Short Mystery Fiction Society's Golden Derringer for Lifetime Achievement and, in 2024, was inducted into the Texas Institute of Letters for his contributions to Texas literature. Learn more at www.crimefictionwriter.com.

www.ingramcontent.com/pod-product-compliance
Lightning Source LLC
Chambersburg PA
CBHW030911060726
47591CB00005B/1498